Darcy and Elizabeth's Valentine's Meet Cute

A PRIDE AND PREJUDICE SHORT STORY

MELISSA ANNE

Copyright © 2024 by Melissa Anne

All rights reserved.

No part of this book may be reproduced in any form or by any electronic or mechanical means, including information storage and retrieval systems, without written permission from the author, except for the use of brief quotations in a book review.

This novel is entirely a work of fiction. The names, characters and incidents portrayed in it are the work of the author's imagination. Any resemblance to actual persons, living or dead, events or localities is entirely coincidental.

This is a work of fiction based on the characters created by Jane Austen in Pride and Prejudice. Ms. Austen created these characters, but like many others, I enjoy placing them in alternate circumstances and situations.

❦ Created with Vellum

For my Family.

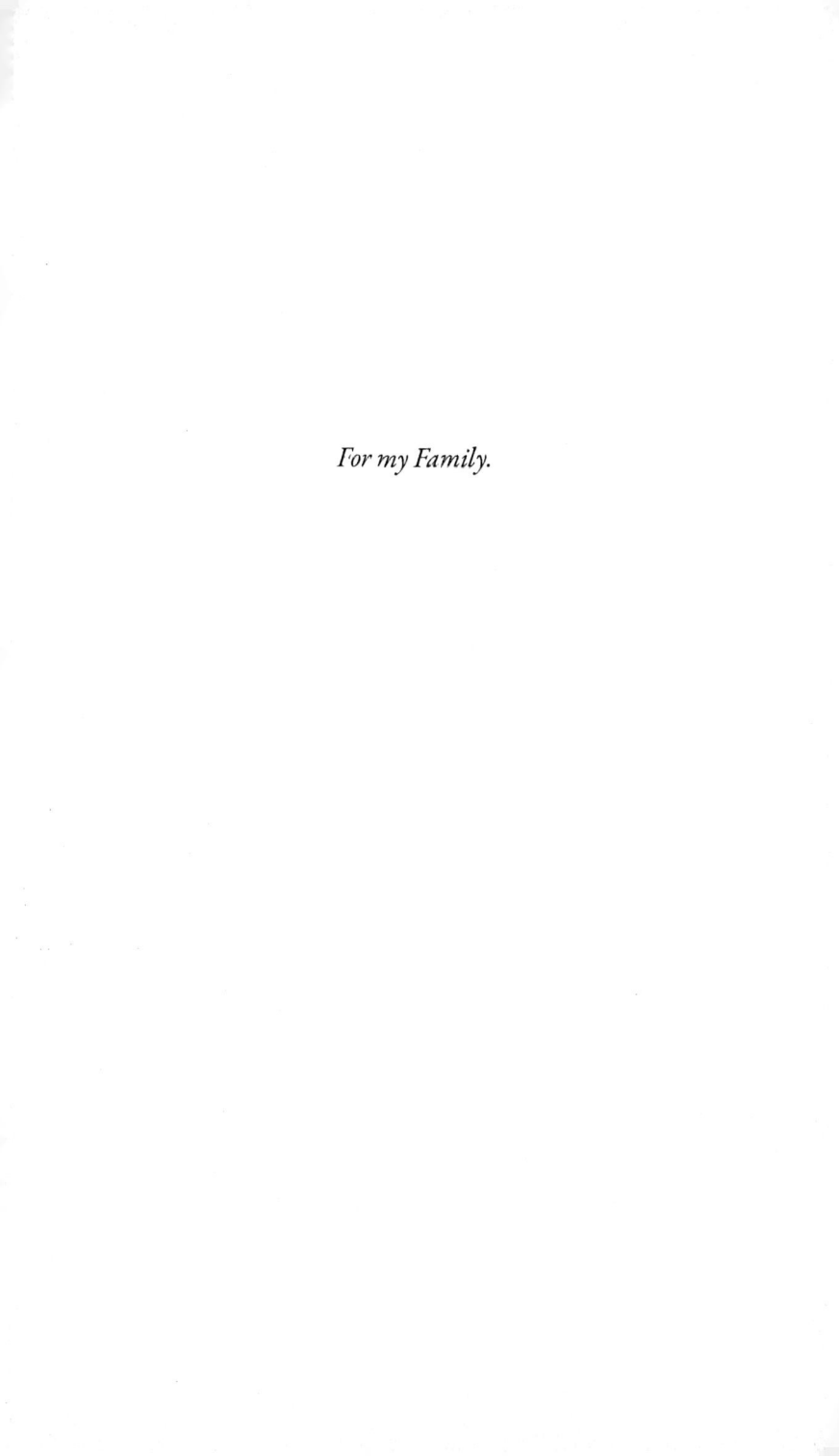

CHAPTER 1

A Chance Meeting

MONDAY 4 FEBRUARY 1811

Fitzwilliam Darcy stepped down from his carriage onto the bustling street before one of his favourite locations in London. Though he often found his time in town tiresome—especially at the height of the Season—there were certain compensations. The theatre, the museums, and, above all, the many bookshops made the experience more tolerable.

On this particular morning, a crisp day in early February, Darcy was in pursuit of books. A message received the day before had informed him that several rare first editions he had long sought had been located. After a brief conversation with Mr. Hatchard, he turned his attention to the shelves, browsing leisurely for other volumes that might capture his interest.

Unbeknownst to him, another patron was also browsing the shelves at Hatchards that morning. As the two strangers wandered through adjacent aisles, they rounded the same corner simultaneously—both engrossed in the books they held and entirely unaware of the other's presence until they collided. Arms full, they stumbled, exclamations escaping their lips as books tumbled to the floor.

"My apologies, madam," Darcy said quickly, his concern evident as he let his own books drop. Instinctively, he reached out, grasping the lady's arms just in time to steady her and prevent a fall.

For a moment, he could do nothing but stare. The lady he had collided with was pretty, though perhaps not in a conventional sense. The delicate imperfections of her face—the slight asymmetry, the uniqueness of her features—only added to her charm. But it was her eyes that held him captive; they were alive with warmth and intelligence, sparkling with amusement as though laughter danced just beneath the surface.

Utterly entranced, he forgot his surroundings, forgot his manners, even forgot the books scattered at their feet.

Despite the abruptness of their meeting, the lady showed no sign of distress or indignation. Many women of his acquaintance would have berated him for his clumsiness—at least until they realised his identity, at which point they might have feigned distress or even claimed to be compromised. Instead, she laughed.

"Well, good morning, sir. I had not realised anyone else was in the shop so early and was not paying attention to where I was going." Her tone was cheerful, entirely free of reproach, and Darcy found himself even more enchanted.

"I believed the same. Might I help you with your books?" Darcy asked, his hands still holding tightly to her arm, though he looked down at the books where they had landed.

She arched an eyebrow at him quizzically. "You would have to release my arms to accomplish that, sir. I believe I have regained my bearings now, and you might allow me to stand on my own." Her grin was infectious, and he found his own growing in response.

"I am pleased that I have not injured you with my inattention. It is not strictly proper for us to introduce ourselves, but might I ask who I have the pleasure of assisting this morning? There is no one else about."

She curtsied puckishly, her eyes flashing with merriment. "I am Miss Elizabeth Bennet, of Longbourn, in Hertfordshire. And might I have the pleasure of knowing who I am addressing?"

"Fitzwilliam Darcy of Pemberley in Derbyshire, at your service, madam," he replied, executing an exaggeratedly gallant bow. As he straightened, he winked at her—an unexpected gesture that sent her into another peal of laughter.

As soon as he straightened from his bow, he bent again to retrieve the scattered books. Elizabeth crouched to assist him, and as they gathered the volumes, their conversation turned naturally to the titles in their hands. Enthralled by their discussion, they lingered there far longer than propriety dictated, neither in any hurry to part ways.

In the midst of the conversation, a voice startled them. "Sir, madam, are you well?" said a clerk as he rounded the corner and saw them both crouched on the ground.

Both flushed as they stood upright, clutching the books. "No, we inadvertently collided with each other and dropped our books. Thank you for your help," Darcy replied, sounding slightly embarrassed to Elizabeth's ears.

She smiled kindly at the clerk, and he stepped away. "Here," she said, holding two titles towards Darcy. "I believe these were yours."

He took the books from her, and their hands touched. The unexpected jolt of energy that seemed to pass between their fingertips startled them both, and their eyes caught and once again locked. "I apologise again, Miss Bennet," he said, his voice deep and grave.

"No need for apologies," she said, sounding breathless. Her eyes sparkled with... something, and Darcy felt himself drawn further under her spell. The two continued to speak of books until Darcy noticed the passing of time.

"Oh, it is getting late. I intended to meet with my solicitor this morning and purchase some new music sheets for Georgiana at the music shop," he exclaimed.

"Is Georgiana your wife?" Elizabeth asked before she could stop herself.

He hid a smirk. "My sister. My much younger sister, as she is only fourteen," he replied quickly, then tilted his head in thought. "In fact, I believe she requires a well-read friend. She has been entirely too interested in novels of late," he said, shuddering theatrically. "Is there any chance I might know your father and could pay a call on him so we can be introduced properly? From our conversation this morning, I think you would be a good friend to my sister." *And I would have a chance to see you again,* he thought.

"My father remains at his estate in Hertfordshire, and since he rarely comes to town, I doubt you know him. I am visiting my uncle, who resides on Gracechurch Street, near Cheapside. He is the owner of Gardiner Exports, and while I know he does business with several gentlemen, I do not know if you would know him," Elizabeth replied, her eyes cast down, wondering if the connection to trade would dissuade the gentleman. She hoped his desire to introduce her to his sister was a mark of interest, at least in knowing her better. While she often read of love at first sight, she had never believed in it before that moment. *It cannot be love, not truly, but attraction. Regardless,* she thought, *I would not wish this to be the last time I see him.*

"Gardiner," Darcy murmured, interrupting her wayward thoughts. "I believe I do know him, or at least, I know of him. My uncle mentioned that name recently and wanted me to meet with him about some investments. I will have to speak to him to find out the details."

"Who is your uncle? I only ask since I have been assisting my uncle occasionally of late, and I know he has several meetings with potential investors soon."

"Henry Fitzwilliam," Darcy replied, giving the name his uncle used when doing business and wished to hide his status as Lord Matlock, the Earl of Matlock.

Elizabeth's eyes widened. "Your uncle is Henry Fitzwilliam?" she asked, aghast. "I apologise, Mr. Darcy, sir, I did not realise. It is *Mr.* Darcy, is it not?" Her emphasis on the Mr. in his name made him realise she knew precisely who his uncle was.

"It is," he replied quietly, seeing the relief in her eyes at his answer.

"I recently had the pleasure of meeting your uncle. He is quite the intriguing character," Elizabeth said shyly.

Darcy chuckled. "That is certainly one way to characterise him. He is a good man, well-versed in many subjects. However, when he is not occupied with matters of Parliament, he tends to be more jovial and personable than serious. Although I only have one other, he is certainly my favourite uncle."

Elizabeth raised an eyebrow, a playful smile tugging at the corners of her lips. "A man of many facets then."

Darcy nodded, his eyes softening as he spoke of his uncle. "Indeed, appearances can be deceiving. He possesses a depth of character that goes beyond the serious demeanour he presents to the world. You would find him enjoying lively discussions, exchanging laughter, and perhaps even engaging in a friendly game or two in his leisure moments."

"We have played a game or two of chess," Elizabeth stated blandly.

It was Darcy's turn to raise an eyebrow. "Who won?" When Elizabeth merely smirked in reply, Darcy's face became incredulous. "You beat him?" he asked.

Elizabeth blushed a little. "Well, I have to admit that we each won a game. We are promised to play again the next time he visits my uncle and has a spare hour or two."

"I will have to ask my uncle about this. He has rarely been beaten—even I, who was a champion at university, have rarely defeated him. I am impressed and hope that I one day have the opportunity to play a game against you," Darcy said, smiling brightly at the woman and now truly intrigued by her.

She smiled, her cheeks flushing once again. "I would enjoy that. But first, you must make the acquaintance of my uncle. And I believe, sir, that you were rushing to depart a little while ago."

He reached for his pocket watch and sighed heavily upon looking at it and confirming the time. "Yes, I truly must leave. How long will you remain in town, Miss Bennet?"

"At least another fortnight, though I hope to stay through Easter. My aunt has promised to take me to a ball; in fact, I believe she promised to take me to the ball hosted by your aunt. It is in ten days, is it not? On St. Valentine's Day?"

"It is. If you attend, I would very much like to reserve a set with you. Perhaps the supper?" he asked.

Her cheeks flamed brightly at that, but she nodded her agreement. "I will save that set for you, sir," she replied quietly. "Now, you must go, else you will be late."

He nodded at her words, then spoke briefly to the clerk, leaving his books on the counter and requesting they be delivered to his house along with the others he had previously discussed with Mr. Hatchard. Before he left, he turned once again to Elizabeth and bowed slightly in farewell. His eyes held hers for another moment until, finally, the door closed behind him.

After meeting with his solicitor, Darcy immediately went to his uncle's house. Unable to banish the woman from his thoughts, even as he attended to his business, he resolved to seek out his uncle and learn more about her.

"You ran into Miss Elizabeth Bennet at Hatchards, most improperly struck up a conversation with her, and now you want to introduce her to your sister? Is there anything else you want to tell me?" Lord Henry Fitzwilliam, Earl of Matlock, boomed in his stentorian voice.

"I asked her to partner with me for the supper set at the ball your wife is hosting on St. Valentine's Day," Darcy informed his uncle. "Originally, I declined the invitation, angering my aunt, but after learning that Miss Bennet will be there, I have changed my mind. Since I know little about her, I have come to see you to ask for more information and to admit to being most intrigued by the lady. I was impressed by her conversation about books and all manner of other things. When she told me she had beaten you at chess, I was astounded and would like to see her play a game just for the novelty of it. A woman who plays chess is uncommon amongst the *ton*, or at least, those who would admit to the accomplishment are even rarer."

Lord Matlock nodded at his nephew, appreciating his forthrightness, nearly chuckling to himself at hearing his nephew speak so of any lady. "Miss Elizabeth Bennet is a most unusual woman. Should you choose in her favour, you would gain a treasure.

"As for her circumstances, I am uncertain of her dowry but would estimate it to be small, if not practically nonexistent. Her most significant connection is her uncle, Edward Gardiner, a man in trade. Though a gentleman, her father owns only a modest estate and, from what his brother reports, is rather indolent in its management, relying heavily on Miss Elizabeth to manage it. The property could be more profitable, but Mr. Bennet lacks the inclination to improve it.

"Since I have had little cause to inquire further, I know little else about the family's affairs, but I can do so if you wish. What I can say with confidence is that Mr. Gardiner is an intelligent man and highly skilled in investments. That was, in fact, my reason for hoping to introduce you to him."

The earl paused in thought before continuing. "I have a meeting with him tomorrow morning. Perhaps you should accompany me. Are you available?"

Darcy nodded. "I will make myself available for the introduction," he replied. Matlock smiled and showed his nephew out.

After this meeting, Darcy returned home, his mind full of Elizabeth Bennet.

CHAPTER 2

Questions

Elizabeth departed Hatchards a few moments after Darcy. She purchased two of the books she had selected, including the one she had discussed with Mr. Darcy since she had been undecided about it until he confirmed its worth. The second was an agricultural treatise her father had requested she purchase, ostensibly for him to read, but in reality, Elizabeth knew she would be the one to read it and then inform her father what it said. Her father loved to read, but he rarely read books on estate matters, preferring Elizabeth to read them and then tell him what he ought to do.

Gratefully, he listened to most of her suggestions, and through this, they had raised the estate's income by twenty-five per cent over the last several years. With luck, this number would continue to increase, for Elizabeth intended to see what she could do to raise her family's fortunes. The excess funds had been turned over to her Uncle Gardiner to invest on behalf of her and her sisters without her mother's knowledge. Longbourn, their estate, was entailed upon the male line, and Elizabeth intended to ensure there were funds to care for her mother and her sisters should their father die before they were all wed. Since there were few men in and around Meryton, the village nearest their estate, it seemed unlikely any would marry well, and it would be unfair to expect whichever sister did marry to care for the rest.

She set the other books she wanted to the side, asking the clerk to hold them for her until the next day since she had only enough funds with her to purchase the two books. Elizabeth hoped she could speak to her aunt about earning a few more coins to purchase the others.

It was generally frowned upon for a gently bred woman to work, but Elizabeth had an arrangement with her aunt that sometimes allowed her to earn a few coins. A few women who worked for her uncle sought to improve their reading and writing skills, and Elizabeth discreetly tutored them in exchange for modest compensation. Her aunt, who managed the household finances skillfully, occasionally found other means for Elizabeth to earn money without compromising her respectability.

Uncle Gardiner could also be counted on to give her a few pounds for assisting him since he relied on her help during her annual visits to town. It was the only time of the year when his office was well organised, and his papers filed correctly. He employed a man for this, but he preferred when Elizabeth did the task, and that was why he convinced her father to send her twice a year for a month or so each time.

As she walked along the bustling streets towards Gracechurch Street, Elizabeth's thoughts kept returning to Mr. Darcy. She had heard his name before, although spoken only in passing. His connection to Lord Matlock intrigued her, especially since the man had not bragged about it, and the way he had spoken of his sister warmed her heart. A man who cared deeply for his family could not be entirely unpleasant despite his somewhat reserved manner.

And then there had been that moment—the brief touch of hands as they exchanged books. Elizabeth shivered even now in memory of it. The sensation had startled her; she had met other gentlemen, yet none had caused such an odd flutter in her chest. But the slightest touch of this man had caused her to feel things she had never felt for any man.

Her aunt greeted her warmly upon her return, quickly noting the distant expression on Elizabeth's face.

"Lizzy, my dear, you seem preoccupied. Was your visit to Hatchards eventful?" her aunt asked kindly, inviting her niece to sit beside her.

Elizabeth hesitated before allowing a small smile and moving to sit on the settee next to her aunt. "You could say that. I had an unexpected encounter with a rather intriguing gentleman."

Mrs. Gardiner's eyes twinkled with alarm. "Indeed? And who might this gentleman be? Did someone accost you? Do I need to send a note to your uncle?"

Elizabeth took a breath, wondering how much to say. "No, Aunt, nothing like that. I...I met Fitzwilliam Darcy of Pemberley. We collided in the bookshop and spoke for a few moments."

Her aunt's brows lifted in surprise. "Mr. Darcy? Now that is interesting."

"You know of him? He said he knew of Uncle," Elizabeth remarked thoughtfully.

"I have heard of him, yes. I grew up in Lambton, which is near his estate of Pemberley. He is considered quite wealthy and is rumoured to be rather reserved, bordering on haughty. But if you have met and liked him, I would rather hear your impression than rely on gossip," Mrs. Gardiner encouraged.

Elizabeth chuckled softly. "His manner is certainly reserved, though not unpleasant or arrogant. He has a dry wit and a great appreciation for books. And he asked for the supper set at Lady Matlock's ball."

Mrs. Gardiner's astonishment was evident. "That is quite a mark of favour, Lizzy."

Elizabeth only smiled in response. His request had also astonished her; the possibility of him changing his mind before the event lingered in the back of her mind. If that happened, she would be disappointed but would not resent him. Their meeting had been unusual, and he might decide that he had acted precipitously.

When Elizabeth did not respond, her aunt laid a hand on her arm. "What is it, Lizzy?" she asked.

"What if he speaks to his uncle and realises I am not worth knowing? I know that Lord Matlock has never met my parents, but what if he tells his nephew that he cannot dance with me because my uncle is in trade? Mr. Darcy is obviously intelligent, his clothes are very fine, and he is related to an earl. He probably is very wealthy, and when he learns I have nothing, he will no longer wish to dance with me. To have asked me for the supper set—he will surely realise he has asked too hastily and will change his mind," Elizabeth said in a rush of words that left her aunt struggling to keep up.

"Stop this, Elizabeth," her aunt scolded. "You cannot assume the worst. Lord Matlock likes you, and I cannot imagine he would warn his nephew off on the sole basis that your uncle is in trade. He has known your uncle for many years and has attempted to introduce your uncle to his nephew on several occasions, but circumstances have always prevented it. I cannot imagine the earl is such a social snob, given that he has dined with us on more than one occasion. And his wife invited us to a ball, which she would not have allowed had she not been pleased to forward the connection."

"Inviting you to a ball is quite different from encouraging a relationship between a tradesman's niece and an earl's nephew," Elizabeth protested, though weakly. However, her aunt's glare silenced any further conversation on the matter.

"What is this about, Elizabeth?" her aunt asked after a moment, her tone gentle.

Elizabeth sighed heavily and slumped back into her seat in an unladylike manner. "I do not know, Aunt—not truly. It was only a brief meeting, yet I... I cannot explain what I felt. I have never experienced anything like it and do not know what to do with myself. And then, for him to have honoured me in such a way—it feels unreal, as though I am in a dream."

Mrs. Gardiner chuckled softly, patting Elizabeth's arm. "You will be well, Lizzy. I believe you have, for the first time, felt a spark of attraction to a man. Something about Mr. Darcy has stirred your heart or mind, and you wish to understand him better. Give it time and see what comes of it. If he seeks you out, you will know he felt something as well," she reassured her niece.

At times, Mrs. Gardiner forgot that, despite Elizabeth's maturity in many ways, she was still quite sheltered—especially regarding matters of the heart.

When Gardiner returned home that afternoon, he was surprised when his wife met him in his study. "Is there something you need, my dear?" he asked, before pulling his wife towards him for a kiss. His wife rarely met him in his study when he arrived home, but he intended to take advantage of it.

They straightened their clothing a few moments later, and Mrs. Gardiner shared her purpose. "Lizzy met Mr. Darcy today at Hatchards. The footman had waited for her outside, so he had little to report, and Lizzy was too unsettled to say much. Suffice it to say, the two introduced themselves and initiated a conversation regarding books. Somehow, it came up that they would both be attending the Matlock's ball on St. Valentine's Day, and Mr. Darcy requested her supper set," Mrs. Gardiner said, placing subtle emphasis on the set he requested.

Gardiner raised his eyebrow. "He is known for avoiding dancing, much less any significant sets. I am uncertain what this may reveal—though it obviously reveals that he wished to spend more time in her presence than a mere dance would have allowed. You will also find it interesting that I received a note from Lord Matlock today informing me that his nephew will accompany him to our meeting tomorrow. Admittedly, that is not strange in and of itself, but I find it telling that he is finally finding the time to join us the day after he met my niece. I will have to speak to Henry privately to see what his nephew might have said.

"Lizzy is concerned he will change his mind about dancing with her once he realises what he has committed himself to.

She did not say as much, but I suspect her mother's comments about her have had more impact than she will admit, even to herself. We will need to encourage her. Now, we had planned to have a new dress made for this ball and ordered one that would have done well enough, but now, I wish to order her a different gown. I already sent a note around to my *modiste* to see if she can work on something different for Lizzy and will pray she can have it ready in time," Mrs. Gardiner said to her husband, kissing him lightly on the chin, as she usually did when she spoke of spending more money than initially planned on a gown.

"If, by some chance, she marries Darcy, we can consider the funds an investment. I know you, Madeline—you would not spend our money frivolously. If you believe this is important, I will not complain," he said, then playfully pinched her bottom and added with a grin, "Too much."

Both husband and wife laughed at his remark, savouring the rare moment of quiet together, free from the company of others.

CHAPTER 3

A Second Meeting

The following day, Darcy presented himself at the address his uncle had given him fifteen minutes before the scheduled appointment. Darcy hated wasting anyone's time, including his own and preferred to arrive at appointments slightly early, allowing time for any obstacles.

Although he arrived at the warehouse early, he still managed to be late for the meeting. While a clerk was escorting him to Gardiner's office, he caught sight of Elizabeth Bennet. She was with a slightly older lady who looked a bit familiar to him, and they seemed to be looking at fabrics.

Asking the clerk to wait a moment, Darcy approached the women. "Miss Bennet, I did not expect to see you today," he said in greeting.

Elizabeth flushed at being caught unaware by the gentleman, and he grinned broadly at her discomposure.

"I was not expecting to see you, sir," she stammered in response, then, after a gentle nudge from her aunt, collected herself enough to do her duty. "Might I introduce you to my aunt, Mr. Darcy?"

At his nod, she performed the introductions. Thankfully, her aunt was more composed and could speak to the gentleman while Elizabeth attempted to gather her wits about her. Finally, her aunt saying her name seemed to bring her back to the conversation.

"...Lizzy or my elder niece Jane often accompany us when we travel. For the last several summers, we have intended to travel to the northern part of the country, but circumstances have prevented it. It will be Lizzy's turn to join us this summer, and I believe she will be delighted to see the Peaks and the Lake District. My husband is uncertain if we will be able to make it so far, but we intend to try," Mrs. Gardiner said.

"Where are you from in Derbyshire, madam?" Darcy asked.

"I grew up in a small village called Lambton," Mrs. Gardiner replied. "I believe you are familiar with it."

Darcy smiled broadly at her. "I am indeed. Lambton is not five miles from Pemberley. It is a delightful village. Miss Bennet, your aunt claims that you enjoy the outdoors; if you are able to join them in travelling to Derbyshire, you absolutely should do so. While I enjoy visiting the Lakes District, I am partial to the Peaks myself, having grown up surrounded by them."

"Oh, I would adore visiting both of those locations. I am afraid my aunt exaggerates how far we have travelled with her, for I have been with her once to Margate, and we were there only a fortnight before Uncle's business recalled him home. Of course, that is farther than most of my sisters have gone, so I should not complain too much, but I have read of too many other places not to wish to travel more frequently. My uncle often allows me to look at his copy of The Universal Atlas and another travel book someone had given him. The illustrations are lovely, but I would adore seeing those places in person one day," Elizabeth replied.

"If you make the journey to Derbyshire, I would be delighted to host your family at Pemberley," Darcy said before turning when he heard his name called. He saw his uncle waving at him and recalled himself to his purpose.

"Forgive me, Miss Bennet and Mrs. Gardiner," he apologised. I arrived early for the meeting but lost track of time speaking to you two ladies. Miss Bennet, I am still looking forward to seeing you at my aunt's ball, but I hope that I will see you before then. Mrs. Gardiner, I enjoyed meeting you and look forward to seeing you again soon."

"Mr. Darcy, you and your uncle would be welcome to join us for dinner one night. Your aunt, too, if she can spare the time, but you would be welcome any time. Please let my husband know if you will come," Mrs. Gardiner said as the gentleman began to leave.

Darcy nodded. "I will need to consult my calendar, but I will send word. Thank you for the invitation," he said before hurrying to where his uncle stood.

"Darcy, nice of you to join us," his uncle said with a knowing look. "How did you find Miss Bennet this morning?"

"Oddly quiet at first, but once Mrs. Gardiner mentioned her niece travelling with her to the Lake District, she became more talkative," Darcy replied, ignoring his uncle's teasing. His ears felt warm, but he hoped his uncle did not notice them growing red.

After a moment passed and no one else spoke, Darcy took the

initiative. "Uncle, perhaps you could introduce me to Mr. Gardiner so we might begin."

Laughing, the earl did as requested, and for the next hour and a half, the three men spoke about various investments. Darcy found Gardiner very knowledgeable and, based on the results his uncle had already seen, elected to invest a substantial amount of money over the coming year.

"Now, Henry, Darcy, my wife informed me that I was to invite the two of you for dinner tonight, and if not tonight, to settle on a date when each of you might come. Of course, if they are available, Henry, your wife, and your sons are also included in the invitation. Darcy, I am told you have a sister who is a few years younger than Lizzy, and she is welcome to join us. But I will leave that up to you," Gardiner said once the business discussion had concluded.

"Your wife mentioned the invitation earlier. I know I have an obligation one night this week, but I cannot recall whether it is tonight or tomorrow. Once I arrive home, I will consult my calendar and send a note," Darcy said before offering his own invitation. "Yesterday, I mentioned to Miss Bennet that I would like to introduce my sister to her, but I am uncertain if dinner would be best. Georgiana can be shy; perhaps a shorter visit in a comfortable location would be better. Perhaps Miss Bennet and Mrs. Gardiner could call at Darcy House one afternoon this week," Darcy suggested.

Both Gardiner and Matlock hid a smile at the invitation, though for different reasons. Matlock knew his niece often suffered from nearly debilitating shyness, and he had long wished to introduce her to Miss Bennet, believing the lively young lady would make an excellent friend. He had not done so before for the same reason that he had never introduced Darcy to Gardiner—simple logistics. Georgiana had rarely been in town at the same time as Miss Bennet, which made the introduction impossible.

However, what amused him even more was Darcy's evident interest in the lady. His nephew had always resisted any matchmaking efforts, whether from himself or his wife, yet here he was, seeking the company of a particular young woman entirely of his own accord.

Gardiner, on the other hand, smiled for an entirely different reason. He had seen how Elizabeth spoke of Mr. Darcy after their meeting—the uncharacteristic hesitations in her words, the thoughtful expression that lingered long after the conversation had ended. Though she likely had not fully admitted it to herself, something about the gentleman had left an impression. His niece was not one to be easily dazzled, and yet there had been a light in her eyes when she recounted their discussion the night before over dinner for Gardiner had inquired minutely into their conversation.

This development intrigued him. Elizabeth had been raised to value intelligence and character over wealth and title, and while Mr. Darcy possessed all four in abundance, his reputation among society was somewhat forbidding. That she had glimpsed something beneath his reserved exterior and that Darcy, in turn, seemed captivated by her was more than enough to make Gardiner curious about what might unfold between them.

Glancing at Matlock, he noted the amusement in the earl's expression and suspected they were thinking along similar lines. Whether this was the beginning of a mere friendship or something more profound, neither man was inclined to interfere—at least, not yet.

Arriving home, Darcy wasted no time discovering that he was expected at a dinner party at his friend Bingley's house that evening. While he liked Bingley well enough, he had little patience for his sisters and brother-in-law. However, when Bingley extended the invitation, he did so with such a hopeful expression that Darcy could not refuse him.

Bingley often reminded Darcy of a puppy—eager to please and too willing to follow the lead of anyone with a stronger will. Unfortunately, this frequently meant he was easily swayed by his younger sister's whims. A year his junior, Caroline Bingley seized every opportunity to exploit her brother's friendship with Darcy, determined to elevate her position through their connection.

Darcy met Bingley during his initial visit to Gentleman Jackson's, a pugilist club favoured by the wealthy and the restless. His cousin, Colonel Richard Fitzwilliam, had dragged him there the day after a particularly trying evening, during which Darcy had nearly been compromised twice by women seeking to entrap him into marriage. Fitzwilliam had believed a bout at the club would improve Darcy's spirits, and in truth, it had—until he noticed Bingley taking a brutal beating from a much larger and far more skilled opponent.

Unable to intervene in the match, Darcy had watched, struck by Bingley's refusal to yield. Though clearly outmatched, he had persisted, enduring blow after blow until he was finally knocked insensible. When no one else stepped forward to assist him, Darcy and Fitzwilliam had taken it upon themselves to see to his care.

Over the following month, the two men had met daily at the club, with Darcy instructing Bingley in the fundamentals he lacked. Fitzwilliam joined them when he could, though his duties to King and Country often occupied him. Through these sessions, a genuine camaraderie had formed, and despite Bingley's occasionally exasperating nature, Darcy had come to regard him with a certain fondness—though he often wished the man were not quite so easily led.

His sisters, however, were another matter entirely. Darcy had little regard for either woman, but from the moment he had met the younger, it had been apparent that she desired him as a husband. While he had no objection to her connections, he did object to her character. Miss Bingley was far haughtier than her position warranted and frequently acted as though she were superior even to those above her in rank. She pretended friendship with Georgiana, but his sister preferred to avoid her whenever possible, for Miss Bingley had a habit of talking over her and disregarding her wishes.

Whenever Darcy was in company with her, Miss Bingley attempted to create an illusion of intimacy between them. She stood too near, took his arm without invitation, and sought to insinuate herself into his social engagements. On more than one occasion, she had arrived at Darcy House uninvited and unexpected, which had led him to cease inviting Bingley to his home altogether. Instead, they met at the club, where Miss Bingley could not intrude. However, he had been unable to decline this particular invitation.

The prospect of enduring Miss Bingley's presumptions that evening was irksome enough. Still, it was all the more aggravating because he could not spend time in Miss Bennet's company until the following evening. With a sigh, he sat at his desk and penned a note to Gardiner, explaining his prior commitment but accepting the invitation for the following evening. He also reiterated his invitation for Miss Bennet and Mrs. Gardiner to call on his sister and, to accommodate their schedule, extended it to any day that week, requesting that they inform him in advance so he could be home to perform the introductions.

CHAPTER 4

Insecurities Arise

Elizabeth had left her uncle's warehouse not long after Darcy's departure. The two spent some time selecting fabrics, with her aunt claiming they would be Christmas gifts for her sisters. Though Elizabeth found it odd to consider Christmas presents in February, she chose not to comment. However, she was too distracted to realise that her aunt's inquiries focused far more on her preferences than those of her sisters.

After leaving the warehouse, they visited the dressmaker they had consulted shortly after the ball, where Elizabeth was to try on the gown for the event. To her surprise, the fitting was brief, with far less attention given to adjustments than expected. Instead, the dressmaker seemed more interested in discussing Elizabeth's tastes and style preferences, much to her confusion.

As the dressmaker draped different fabrics over Elizabeth's arm and held up lace and ribbons in various shades, her aunt watched with a smile. Elizabeth, however, remained oblivious to the true purpose of their visit. She answered each question distractedly, her thoughts still lingering on Mr. Darcy.

When the dressmaker inquired whether Elizabeth preferred a richer jewel-toned fabric or something softer, she hesitated before murmuring something about preferring practicality. Mrs. Gardiner chuckled and exchanged a knowing look with the seamstress.

"My dear, a well-chosen gown is not an extravagance but a necessity," her aunt said gently. "And I should like to see you in something that brings out the colour in your cheeks."

Elizabeth glanced down at the fabric in her hands—a deep emerald green that was far more striking than anything she would have chosen for herself. She opened her mouth to protest but closed it again when she caught her aunt's expression. There was something in Mrs. Gardiner's eyes—perhaps anticipation or a quiet kind of determination.

"Aunt, I cannot help but notice that you seem to have taken an unusual interest in my wardrobe today," Elizabeth remarked, arching an eyebrow. "What are you about?"

Mrs. Gardiner merely smiled. "I wish for you to look your best, Lizzy. After all, you never know what opportunities might arise where you will need a new gown."

Elizabeth narrowed her eyes slightly at the comment but chose to continue as she had. The rest of the visit passed quickly, and before too much longer, they had returned home.

That afternoon, she joined the children on their daily walk to the park. It was unseasonably warm, so they spent a little over an hour playing games and enjoying the fresh air. Elizabeth delighted in watching her young cousins chase one another through the grass, their laughter ringing out frequently. She joined them in a game of hide-and-seek, much to their amusement, and finally in a game of hoops. Tired and slightly red-faced, all four of them, together with the nursemaid and governess, trooped back to the Gardiner home, having enjoyed the afternoon.

"You seem in good spirits today, Lizzy," her aunt remarked when she entered the house, her voice tinged with amusement.

Elizabeth turned to her aunt with an easy smile. "It is difficult not to be in good spirits, Aunt. The weather is fine, the children are happy, and I have little reason for complaint."

After indicating that Elizabeth should sit, Mrs. Gardiner poured her niece a cup of tea and quietly fixed it, giving her time to recover after such an active afternoon with her cousins. Once Elizabeth was settled again, Mrs. Gardiner arched a brow, her expression knowing. "And seeing Mr. Darcy this morning has nothing to do with your pleasant mood?"

A flush crept up Elizabeth's neck as she struggled to frame a response. "I very much enjoyed my time with the children," she replied, focusing intently on her teacup.

Mrs. Gardiner merely hummed in amusement but said no more. Instead, she reached for a folded note resting beside her on the table. "Edward sent this earlier," she said, holding it up for Elizabeth. "Mr. Darcy has accepted the dinner invitation for tomorrow night and reiterated his offer for us to call on Darcy House at our convenience. We need only decide on a suitable day."

Attempting to appear indifferent, Elizabeth took a measured sip of her tea, but the warmth lingering in her cheeks betrayed her. "That is very kind of him. I suppose we should determine which day is best."

Mrs. Gardiner hid a smile behind her cup. "Indeed. I would like to see his home, and I would like to meet Miss Darcy. I wonder if she takes after her mother. I saw Lady Anne once or twice when I was in Lambton—she knew my mother—but our paths did not cross often."

Tracing the rim of her saucer with one finger, Elizabeth hesitated. "I do not wish to impose upon him. We only met yesterday, though he must be serious about introducing me to his sister. He extends the invitation so frequently that I can only assume she desperately needs a friend."

Setting her cup down, Mrs. Gardiner regarded her niece with amusement and knowing affection. "Elizabeth, my dear, I suspect the invitation is as much about him seeing you in his home as it is about you meeting his sister. While Miss Darcy may very well need a friend, I do not doubt that he wishes for your presence there just as much—if not more."

"Aunt," Elizabeth protested once more.

"I know, Lizzy, and I do not mean to meddle," she said. "However, the man has shown a particular interest in you, and you have only seen him twice. How many times has he suggested you visit? He is coming here for dinner tomorrow night."

"If he were as anxious as you think, why is he waiting until tomorrow to come? Why is he not coming tonight?" Elizabeth asked, thinking she would make this point against her aunt.

"Because he has a prior commitment this evening," Mrs. Gardiner retorted. "Even still, he is gracious in allowing us time to prepare for his company. He is not waiting for his other family but is coming alone because he wishes to see you."

Elizabeth conceded that her aunt may have a point, but she still attempted to keep her hopes in check. She did not want to be disappointed and was still not entirely convinced that the gentleman could genuinely be interested in her.

Elizabeth sat in her room the next morning, reflecting on why she was in London. As the second of five daughters, she had always been closest to her elder sister, Jane. Lately, however, that bond had frayed, prompting Elizabeth to seek a closer friendship with Mary instead.

When a young gentleman leased Netherfield last autumn, he initially showed great interest in Jane. Over time, however, his attention shifted towards Elizabeth. She had thought little of it at first, as she had primarily accompanied Jane as a chaperone rather than an equal participant. Always reserved in unfamiliar company, Jane spoke little beyond the expected pleasantries, leaving Elizabeth to sustain the conversation.

It was only when the gentleman—if one could call him that—prepared to leave that his true nature became evident. With self-important arrogance, he informed them that, between them, they made the perfect woman—one possessing beauty, the other intelligence.

The remark had offended them both. Elizabeth, quick-witted as ever, had given him a scathing reply, but the damage was done. Instead of condemning the man's rudeness, Jane turned her disappointment on Elizabeth, convinced that her impertinence had driven him away. From that moment, a rift grew between them—one Elizabeth, despite her best efforts, had been unable to mend.

This fracture in their relationship was why Elizabeth accompanied her aunt and uncle to London after Christmas and remained there still. Their mother, siding with Jane's account, had been furious, blaming Elizabeth entirely for chasing off a potential suitor. In a fit of temper, she even wished to send Elizabeth away permanently. Disinclined to refuse his wife in most matters, Mr. Bennet would not allow the banishment, but he did agree to an extended visit with the Gardiners, reasoning that time apart might ease tensions.

Though he was displeased by his favourite daughter's prolonged absence, he had, as ever, chosen the path of least resistance. With few pressing matters of business during the winter months, he left matters to his steward and sought the peace that eluded Longbourn when household squabbles arose.

All of this left Elizabeth uncertain about her place in the world. Her father and Jane's suitor had valued her intelligence, yet it had not been enough—her father did not seek her company, nor had Jane's suitor fallen in love with her. Her mother, meanwhile, openly favoured Jane for her beauty and Lydia for her liveliness, finding little in Elizabeth to praise. She considered Elizabeth's love of books and learning unnatural and frequently criticised her appearance.

Where Jane was blonde, blue-eyed, and took after their mother, Elizabeth had dark hair and green eyes and bore a stronger resemblance to the Bennet family. Jane was tall and slender, while Elizabeth's figure was more voluptuous. Though Elizabeth frequently walked out—another habit her mother disapproved of—it did nothing to change her looks.

Though many in Meryton called her the second most beautiful Bennet daughter, such compliments were never echoed at Longbourn.

It was little wonder, then, that Elizabeth struggled to believe Mr. Darcy could truly be interested in her. As she anxiously awaited his visit for dinner that evening, doubt gnawed at her.

"What is the matter, Lizzy?" Mrs. Gardiner asked when Elizabeth came downstairs, her eyes dull from lack of sleep.

"I have merely been thinking, Aunt," Elizabeth began, her voice faltering slightly. She sighed deeply before sitting beside Mrs. Gardiner, whose counsel she had always held in high regard.

Mrs. Gardiner looked at her with gentle encouragement. "What about, my dear?" she prompted softly, her eyes warm and understanding. Having known Elizabeth for over a decade and having spent enough time at Longbourn to witness the dysfunction of that household, Mrs. Gardiner knew her niece was troubled but preferred to let Elizabeth voice her concerns in her own time. Mrs. Gardiner suspected it had something to do with Mr. Darcy's attention, and she knew it was only a matter of time before Elizabeth would open up.

After a pause, Elizabeth hesitated, clearly struggling with her thoughts. At last, she spoke, her voice quiet but earnest. "I have been thinking about Mr. Darcy," she admitted, gazing downward. "You said that his asking me to dance is a mark of his interest, and while I was pleased when he first asked, I now feel I should decline."

"Why do you believe so?" Mrs. Gardiner asked, trying to understand her niece's reasoning.

Elizabeth paused, staring into the small fire burning in the grate for several moments before answering, her voice tinged with a hint of sorrow. "There seems little point in encouraging any expectations or in allowing others to speculate about our connection. I know that nothing will come of it. A man like Mr. Darcy cannot truly be interested in someone like me—a country girl with nothing to offer. He would much rather be seen with a beauty like Jane, someone who possesses the grace and charm of the accomplished young ladies he is accustomed to. A dance with someone like me, Aunt... well, it seems absurd." Her voice wavered, and frustration and sadness shimmered in her eyes, betraying the emotions she struggled to contain.

Mrs. Gardiner sat silently, taking in her niece's words. She had always seen Elizabeth as a young woman of sharp intelligence and lively spirit, qualities that made her stand out far more than her niece was willing to admit. But she knew Elizabeth's heart was tender and that she carried the weight of her own doubts more heavily than most, in large part due to an indolent father and an overly critical mother.

"Elizabeth," she began softly, "you are a woman of rare worth and must not undervalue yourself. Mr. Darcy may be a man of high station, but it *is* possible he is truly interested in you. Do not be so quick to dismiss the attention he has paid to you. He has been out in society for many years and has likely encountered many women like Jane, who society claims are beautiful. But neither of your parents has ever complimented you, and you likely do not realise how beautiful you are in your own right. You are intelligent and witty, and it seems likely that Mr. Darcy would admire you for those qualities."

Elizabeth shook her head, her expression tight with uncertainty. "I want to believe that, Aunt. I do. But I cannot ignore what I know. Men like Mr. Darcy—wealthy, accomplished, and used to the finest of society—surely would not look for affection from someone like me. And while I would never claim that my sisters are without merit, I cannot help but see how little I measure up to them in his eyes. Jane is everything a man like him could desire. I... I am not."

Mrs. Gardiner reached out and took Elizabeth's hand, her touch gentle but firm. "You have more strength and grace than you give yourself credit for. And I believe Mr. Darcy sees that, even if you do not yet see it yourself. Do not reject his overtures simply because you think you cannot compare. He has asked you to dance the supper set, meaning he wants to spend more than half an hour in your company."

Elizabeth looked up at her aunt, her face clouded with doubt, but her heart felt slightly lighter. She longed to believe her aunt's words, but the fear of disappointment held her back. While she wanted others to see her for who she truly was and desired a marriage of equals for genuine affection, she wondered if that was what Mr. Darcy would wish. The thought of him paying her any real attention seemed impossible. And yet... there was a small, vulnerable part of her that dared to hope.

"I shall think on your words, Aunt," Elizabeth whispered. "But for now, I cannot help but feel I am not meant for such attentions. What if he sees Jane and changes his mind, or another woman whom he prefers."

Mrs. Gardiner smiled gently. "Perhaps, my dear, the greatest mistake is to assume we are not worthy of what we deserve. Mr. Darcy's actions may surprise you yet. Do not be too quick to judge what you do not fully understand."

Elizabeth nodded, but the uncertainty remained in her heart. Still, her aunt's words lingered in her mind, planting a small seed of doubt in her own resolve. Perhaps there was more to Mr. Darcy's regard than she had allowed herself to believe.

CHAPTER 5

Dinner at the Gardiners

Darcy's palms were slick with sweat as he sat in his carriage on the way to dinner at the Gardiner residence. After entering the vehicle, he had removed his gloves and absentmindedly wrung them in his hands as the horses clopped along the cobbled streets. Realising he was fidgeting uncharacteristically, he set the gloves beside him on the seat, only to find that now his hands felt even more restless.

He glanced out the window, watching the passing cityscape to calm his thoughts. Despite the constant movement of the carriage, it felt as though time had slowed, each second stretching longer than the last. It was a familiar sensation—one he had often experienced before an event that had the potential to unsettle him—though he could not entirely pinpoint why this particular evening was causing such unease.

Darcy had anticipated seeing Miss Bennet soon but had not expected Mrs. Gardiner to issue a dinner invitation so quickly nor for Mr. Gardiner to second it. He knew the invitation aimed to throw him and Miss Bennet together, and for the first time, he did not mind being nudged toward a young woman. Though their two interactions had been brief, her presence had lingered in his mind.

Darcy exhaled slowly, trying to steady himself. It was only a dinner. Nothing more.

However, his nervousness returned as he recalled the conversation with his cousin earlier that afternoon. As he often did, Fitzwilliam had barged into his study unannounced, a grin already playing across his face. Darcy had been engrossed in a letter when Fitzwilliam arrived, and it did not take long for him to launch into one of his usual, incessant rounds of questioning.

"Well, Darcy," Fitzwilliam began, a teasing tone in his voice. I have it on excellent authority that a young lady has entirely captured your interest. She must be quite the paragon."

Darcy had been momentarily taken aback, his pen stilling in his hand. "I have no idea what you mean."

Determined to tease, Fitzwilliam crossed the room to sit across from him, his smirk widening. "Oh, come now, Darcy. My father mentioned something about you calling on him yesterday to ask about a young lady, and I thought you might be willing to share a bit more with me. Who is she, then? Surely, you must have some idea of what you are doing when you call on her."

Darcy had narrowed his eyes slightly, unsure how much to reveal. He had never been one to indulge in the kind of conversation Fitzwilliam was aiming for, yet there was no avoiding it now. He could feel his cousin's energy crackling in the air, ready to pounce on whatever morsel of information he could extract.

Reluctantly, Darcy sighed, his shoulders stiff. "I met the young lady at Hatchards the day before yesterday. Her name is Elizabeth Bennet, and she is Mr. Gardiner's niece."

At the mere mention of her name, Fitzwilliam's grin had grown. "Mr. Gardiner? The tradesman who Father does business with? You are considering attaching yourself to the daughter of a tradesman? She must have quite the dowry if you are considering her."

"I know nothing of her dowry and have only spoken to her twice. I am dining at her uncle's house after he and I met yesterday with your father to discuss my joining his investment. Your father has done very well with Mr. Gardiner, and I intend to do the same," Darcy said in an attempt to redirect his cousin. It was not successful.

"Ah, now I understand," Fitzwilliam had said, his eyes gleaming. "You are investing with the uncle to impress the girl. You must be genuinely interested in her. Is she a beauty?"

Darcy had flinched at his cousin's probing, but there was little point in denying his feelings. "She is... an intriguing young woman," he had admitted reluctantly, unwilling to go further.

"Intriguing?" Fitzwilliam had raised an eyebrow. "That's it? My dear cousin, you must have more to say than that! Come now, do not be so modest. Tell me—what is it you find so fascinating about her to cause you to speak to my father and seek her out?"

Darcy was struggling his attraction to the lady and was not quite ready to express his feelings to anyone, but Fitzwilliam was relentless.

"What I find most interesting about her," Darcy said slowly, searching for the right words, "is her independence and wit.

She is not one simply to agree with everything I say. She challenges my assumptions, and I find that refreshing."

"Ah!" Fitzwilliam exclaimed as if the conversation had finally reached the point he had been waiting for. "A woman who speaks her mind! I see now. Darcy, my friend, you must act on this."

Darcy had been about to protest—there were many reasons why acting on these impulses was not a good idea—but Fitzwilliam had not given him a chance.

"Listen, Darcy," Fitzwilliam had said, leaning forward with an eager gleam in his eyes. "You cannot simply admire her from a distance. You must take action. Show her that you are a man of action. Call on her. Invite her to dine at Darcy House. Be decisive! If she has captured your attention, she must be worthy."

Darcy had straightened in his chair, half-annoyed and half-bewildered. "Fitzwilliam, I do not *court* women in such a manner. I do not see the need to... act impulsively in this matter."

But Fitzwilliam had only waved away his concerns. "That is your problem, Darcy—you think too much. A little spontaneity will do you good."

Darcy had shaken his head, trying to suppress a smile at his cousin's insistence. "And what would you suggest I do, Fitzwilliam? Write her a sonnet?"

Fitzwilliam had burst out laughing at the suggestion, but he had not stopped his pursuit. "Perhaps not a sonnet, but something more practical. Take her to the theatre, or invite her to walk through the park, something that will give you a chance to speak with her, to... get to know her. You obviously enjoy her company."

The idea of being alone with Elizabeth and speaking with her freely and without the walls of propriety or formality both intrigued and unsettled Darcy. Fitzwilliam's suggestions only reminded him how little control he had over the situation.

Before he had time to further process Fitzwilliam's relentless suggestions, his cousin slapped him on the back with exaggerated cheer. "You have nothing to lose, Darcy! Show her the man you truly are. You may find she appreciates the effort."

The conversation lingered in Darcy's mind, and any number of unanswered questions swirled through his thoughts as the carriage began to slow. Would he take Fitzwilliam's advice and act spontaneously? He had already done so by asking her to dance the supper set. He laughed to himself; he realised he had not mentioned that to his cousin. Without a doubt, Fitzwilliam would not have ceased his teasing had he mentioned it.

Upon entering the house, Darcy immediately went to Elizabeth's side after greeting his host and hostess.

"Miss Bennet, how are you this evening?" he inquired.

"I am very well, Mr. Darcy," she replied, her cheeks tinged with pink. "My aunt told me that we will be visiting your sister tomorrow. I am looking forward to meeting her."

"Yes, she sent me a note earlier telling me the same," he said. "I have told my sister to expect callers tomorrow, but I am afraid she is anxious about the visit. She is worried that you and your aunt will be more along the lines of my friend's sisters, and she always dreads their visits. I have attempted to cease their calls, but they can be relentless. However, I feel certain you will quickly put her at ease as you did with me." His eyes were warm, and Elizabeth's cheeks flushed again at the compliment.

Immediately trying to regain her composure, Elizabeth opted to tease the gentleman.

"What sort of sisters does your friend have, Mr. Darcy?" she asked, laughing lightly.

"They sound as though they must be quite fearsome."

Darcy chuckled at the thought. "Fearsome is not quite the right word, but I am not certain of a better one. My friend, Charles Bingley, and I are opposites in many ways, but we have become rather friendly over the last two years. However, he has a younger sister who has made it her mission to become Mrs. Darcy. Her actions often make me uncomfortable, and I am never quite certain how to deal with her."

"For instance," he continued, "last night, I was invited to a dinner party at their home, which turned out to be a meal with her family and me. The whole situation was uncomfortable, especially since she seated me on her right as the guest of honour and then attempted to monopolise my attention all evening. It would be ungentlemanly of me to correct her behaviour, yet despite my hints to her brother, he has not done so."

"On seven occasions, I have tried to indicate that I do not appreciate her grabbing my arm every time we are in company, especially when it is not offered, but she cannot seem to understand that. Her brother claims she simply refuses to listen to any suggestions he gives her about her behaviour towards me or that an invitation is not meant to include her."

"And so," Darcy sighed, "I have stopped inviting him to my home and instead always opt to see him at my club."

Elizabeth chuckled. "And at your club, no women are allowed, so she cannot join him there. I would guess she is rather displeased at this change in your behaviour."

Darcy smiled slightly. "Very much, but I have no intention of doing anything else," he said. "Now, let us speak of something more agreeable."

Darcy then asked Elizabeth about the books she had purchased at Hatchards the morning they met. They began discussing those books along with several others. Darcy was intrigued that the lady read books about agriculture to assist her father with his estate. He was further interested when she mentioned other purchases, including a volume of Cowper and another by Wordsworth.

"What did you think of *The Lady of the Lake*?" he asked.

"Oh, I found it most enjoyable," she replied. "I have read it already twice and hope to read it a third time. It is such an interesting tale."

Darcy could do little but agree. Before either of them realised it, dinner was announced.

Mr. Gardiner escorted his wife into the dining room, leaving Darcy to escort Miss Bennet. Once again, even through the layers of clothing, Darcy felt Elizabeth's touch like a lightning bolt to his heart. It was an odd sensation, unlike anything he had ever felt.

At dinner, the conversation was more general, and all four diners participated. The topics ranged from politics (with frequent news about the Regent and his excesses) to matters of fashion (which were of less interest to the gentlemen, but they indulged the women in speaking of which muslin was best). Finally, they discussed the investment Darcy had agreed to the previous day.

Darcy was surprised at the breadth and depth of knowledge of his host and hostess, and of course, Miss Bennet was likewise delightful.

When the final course was served and the table cleared, Mrs. Gardiner stood. She and Elizabeth left the room to allow the gentlemen a few minutes alone. Once the door shut behind her, Mr. Gardiner spoke to Darcy.

"Mr. Darcy, I realise that we only met yesterday, and this is your third meeting with my niece. However, given the difference in your statuses, I would like to ask, what are your intentions towards her? Elizabeth is a wonderful young lady, and we treasure her, but I would not have you toying with her affections."

Darcy was a little surprised at the directness with which Mr. Gardiner spoke to him, but as he considered it momentarily, he appreciated the concern. It was clear that he cared for his niece deeply and wished the best for her. He would likely do the same thing if someone began paying attention to his sister.

"I cannot say fully what my intentions are now," Darcy began, "but I would like to get to know Miss Bennet better. As you said, we have only met three times, but I have enjoyed speaking with her each time. We have never run out of things to talk about. She is unlike any woman I have ever met, and I have been out in society for more than five years. Quite a few fathers and mothers have courted me, and I have been in danger of being compromised a time or two by unscrupulous women, but I have always managed to avoid such actions. However, your niece intrigues me, and while I cannot commit to a courtship or a proposal at this moment, given the brief time of our acquaintance, I would like to see where things go between us."

Mr. Gardiner nodded. "So, your intentions are honourable?" he asked to clarify.

"Certainly, sir," Darcy replied. "I would not toy with anyone's affections. However, I also truly wish for her to befriend my sister. Regardless of what may happen between Miss Bennet and myself, she has a lively character that I think my sister needs. I myself am rather reticent, and my sister is almost painfully shy. A woman like Miss Bennet might assist her in bringing her out of her shell, and I feel that she will be honest with my sister and not attempt to use her relationship with her to forward her acquaintance with me."

Mr. Gardiner seemed to consider this for a moment. "Tell me more about your sister," he said.

"Georgiana is young—soon to be fifteen. I have a companion for her, but she is an older woman, and I am not always certain how well she and Georgiana get along. In some ways, it seems Mrs. Younge is leading Georgiana and directing her, which is as it should be, but it sometimes seems that Mrs. Younge ignores Georgiana's wishes in favour of her own. I cannot be certain since Georgiana will say nothing negative about her, but I feel that the woman is hiding something. Although I cannot put my finger on precisely what it is. I hope that perhaps your wife and niece can observe the interactions as well, for I do not think she behaves in the same manner when I am in the room as she does when she is alone with Georgiana."

"If you do not trust the woman," Mr. Gardiner said, "why do you not discharge her and find a new companion?"

Darcy sighed. "I wish it were that simple. Since my Aunt Catherine recommended her to me, I cannot dismiss her without a valid reason."

"Why is that?" Mr. Gardiner asked.

Darcy groaned. "In part because my aunt will never let me hear the end of it if I dismiss a worthy employee without cause. That I have a bad feeling about her—or not even a bad feeling, just a suspicion that all is not as it should be—would be enough to bring my aunt from Kent to London to berate me. Of course, she may do so if I dismiss the lady with cause, but at least then, I will have more than a feeling to back my reasoning. Perhaps I should worry less about what my aunt thinks, but family can be difficult."

Mr. Gardiner had to laugh. "You are correct about that. I should warn you that if you are interested in my niece, you should know about her parents. I have told Lord Matlock before that my brother is far more indolent than he ought to be, which is a matter of contention between Bennet and me. For years, I tried speaking to him and encouraging him to invest so his daughters would have a proper dowry, but he refuses to do any more than what Elizabeth has already done for him. You should know that Lizzy, should you decide in her favour, will come to you with practically nothing. Despite her efforts, she has only saved a few hundred pounds each year for the last three years since she began assisting with its management. Given what I know about you after our meeting yesterday, I doubt that will be a problem for you, but you should know it."

"Her mother, however, is another matter entirely," Mr. Gardiner continued. "Her mother is my sister, and Fanny often acts more like a spoiled child than a grown woman. Lizzy is in London with my wife and me because Fanny blames her for running off a suitor for her elder daughter, Jane. The young man informed the two girls that together, they were ideal, for one had beauty and the other had brains. Each was offended, but Jane preferred to blame Lizzy for his defection. It seems Jane would not speak to the gentleman, so Lizzy did, and that was enough for her sister to fault her.

"My sister's main goal is to marry off her daughters, although she is convinced that only her oldest and youngest will marry well. They are most like her in looks and spirit, and the rest take after their father in appearance, so she dismisses them. She is highly critical of Lizzy, and this is not the first time she has come to London to escape her."

Darcy considered this for a moment. "You are not the only one who has difficult relatives. As I mentioned, my aunt, Lady Catherine de Bourgh, can be quite the harridan." He sighed heavily and then continued. "Since my father's death, she had attempted to claim that she and my mother engaged me to my cousin when we were both in our cradles. There was never any mention of this before both my parents were gone. My cousin is sickly and cross, and even if she were inclined to wed, I would refuse to marry her simply because my aunt insists it is so. Even if it was discussed, our fathers never signed a contract. While my mother might have thought it a good idea when we were infants, I do not think she would wish it today. Regardless of how often I have told my aunt otherwise, she continues to insist. Should I engage myself to your niece, I do not doubt she would attempt to claim I am obligated to Anne."

"Ha!" Gardiner exclaimed. "Is this, by chance, your uncle's sister?"

Darcy smiled. "It is."

"Then I will need to tease him about it sometime. He insists his family is nearly perfect, and now I know his secret."

Darcy laughed at this. "You have not met his second son, Colonel Fitzwilliam, then have you? He certainly gives lie to that claim."

The gentlemen then left the dining room and joined the ladies in the parlour. Elizabeth was at the piano, lightly playing as her aunt sewed, and Darcy immediately approached her.

"Might I turn the pages for you, Miss Bennet?" Darcy asked. At Elizabeth's nod, he sat on the bench beside her.

"Mr. Darcy," Elizabeth whispered, and then hesitated.

"Yes," he prompted, hoping she would continue. He thought she looked troubled and wondered what he could do to relieve her worry.

She sighed. "Your asking me for the supper set at your aunt's ball—it was done impulsively, was it not?"

"It was," he replied and watched her visibly deflate. "But that does not mean that I did not mean it or wish to retract it. When I heard you would attend, I looked forward to spending more time with you. The supper set allows me to not only get a half hour with you while dancing, but it also enables me to sit next to you throughout the supper."

"But my aunt says you do not dance often. Our dancing together might be remarked on," she whispered.

He barked a laugh and attempted to cover it with a cough. "It most certainly will. Does that trouble you?" he asked, his brow furrowing.

"I do not wish to embarrass you," she replied.

"You could not. I will be honoured to dance with you and to be able to claim a significant amount of your time that evening. In fact, I had considered asking your uncle if I could escort you to the ball so I can keep you on my arm whenever you are not dancing with another," he whispered.

"You cannot mean that," she hissed, her mind racing. If Darcy escorted her, there would be no hiding from the whispers, the watchful eyes. Although the thought made her nervous, she could not deny the thrill of the idea—of being by his side, of him making his interest so very clear.

"Why ever not?" he asked, confused by her response.

Elizabeth looked away, her fingers tightening around the edges of her shawl. "Because it would give rise to speculation. People will talk and wonder why you are dancing with me. I am a nobody, a country miss with practically no dowry and connections to trade."

Darcy studied her carefully, his expression unreadable. "They will talk regardless, Miss Bennet." His voice softened as he leaned in. "Would it truly be so terrible if they assumed I hold you in special regard?"

Her breath caught. "But do you?" She wished the words back at once.

He exhaled, his gaze intense. "Yes."

She blinked, her heart hammering in her chest. He had answered without hesitation, without pretence. It left her feeling both exhilarated and unsettled. "Oh," she murmured, unable to form a more coherent reply.

A slow, knowing smile curved his lips. "This is only the third time we have met, so I am not ready to speak to your uncle, but I would like to continue calling on you. I look forward to introducing you to my sister, and I cannot help but feel that you will become special to the both of us. My sister will like you very much, and I hope you will inspire her confidence. I would not want to introduce you if I did not think you were worth knowing."

Elizabeth smiled, though her thoughts still swirled. He was unlike any gentleman she had ever known—direct, sincere, and apparently unwilling to play society's usual games. It was both refreshing and disarming, and she contemplated this as she continued playing a simple piece she did not need music for.

She swallowed hard. "You are very determined, sir," she said finally.

He chuckled. "You have no idea, Miss Bennet."

Elizabeth played a short time longer before the couple joined her aunt and uncle across the room. As they had done during the meal, the four talked pleasantly together and enjoyed conversation until it grew late.

"I think I must go," Darcy finally said. "I look forward to you calling at my house tomorrow, Miss Bennet, Mrs. Gardiner.

Both ladies noticed that Darcy often addressed Elizabeth first, which was not what propriety would have dictated, but it made Darcy's focus clear.

At her aunt's urging, Elizabeth showed Darcy to the door.

"I thank you for a pleasant evening, Mr. Darcy," she said as he donned his hat, coat, and gloves.

"I look forward to many more," he murmured. "I will see you tomorrow, Miss Bennet," he repeated, taking Elizabeth's hand and pressing a light kiss to the back.

Elizabeth flushed, causing Darcy to grin as he nodded at her and exited the front door. She stood there watching him for several moments, her cheeks heating further when he glanced out the window of his carriage and caught her watching him. Instead of joining her aunt and uncle in the parlour, she called out a goodnight before making her way to her room where she could think.

CHAPTER 6

Meeting Georgiana

When she and her aunt arrived at Darcy House promptly at eleven, Elizabeth's nerves were already high. But the sight of the grand townhouse only stirred her insecurities anew.

Before she could step out of the carriage, her gaze met Darcy's. He had spotted their arrival from his study window and hurried outside to greet them.

"Miss Bennet, Mrs. Gardiner, welcome to Darcy House," he said as they stepped onto the pavement. He offered his arm to Mrs. Gardiner, but she declined, allowing Elizabeth to take it instead.

His attention sent warmth to her cheeks, and she lowered her eyes, focusing on her steps as they climbed the stairs to enter the house.

Stepping inside, Elizabeth took in the house's elegance with quiet astonishment. Beside her, Darcy seemed to notice her uncharacteristic silence and wondered about it. His own anxiety over introducing Elizabeth to his sister grew as well.

Elizabeth did not seem to notice the servants who took away her bonnet and cloak, nor when Darcy led her up the stairs to lead her to the library on the first floor. Instead of escorting the ladies into the drawing room where Georgiana awaited them, he turned instead into the library.

"Miss Bennet, are you well?" he asked quietly. Mrs. Gardiner stood to the side, having noticed her niece's obvious discomposure and hoping the gentleman would be able to answer her far better than she would.

Elizabeth closed her eyes and took a moment to collect herself. "Forgive me, Mr. Darcy. I am overwhelmed by seeing your house for the first time and trying to remind myself of both my aunt's words and those you said last evening."

"It is just a house, Miss Bennet," Darcy said, trying to tease the lady a little, hoping it would alleviate some of her concerns.

"Your townhouse is nearly as large as the manor on my father's estate," Elizabeth retorted.

Mrs. Gardiner laughed lightly. "You exaggerate, Lizzy, my dear. Longbourn is quite a bit larger. Perhaps not as fine," she trailed off as she took in the room they had entered.

"Papa would swoon if he ever saw this," Elizabeth chuckled, her nerves beginning to leave her. "He would never wish to leave."

"Are you recovered, Miss Bennet?" Darcy asked, smiling at her fondly.

"Yes," she replied, looking at him directly in his eyes for the first time. "Forgive my foolishness."

Darcy chuckled slightly. "There is nothing to forgive, Miss Bennet. Come, let me introduce you to my sister."

The introduction was less anticlimactic than Elizabeth might have thought. Georgiana was at first so shy that she barely spoke and certainly could not hold anyone's eye for more than a moment. However, Elizabeth was gentle with her. Mrs. Gardiner sat at a distance and spoke quietly with Mr. Darcy while Mrs. Younge sat in a corner, looking at the visitors with a disapproving gaze. Darcy did not notice it, being caught up in watching his sister and Elizabeth, but Mrs. Gardiner did.

Having been warned by her husband of what to look for, she observed the companion nearly as closely as she did her niece and Miss Darcy. It was clear that Mrs. Younge did not appreciate this new friend, but Mrs. Gardiner could not be sure what the lady's objection might be.

After nearly half an hour and once Georgiana had become more comfortable with Elizabeth's presence, Darcy felt comfortable leaving the ladies to continue to speak while he attended to business in his study. "Stay as long as you like, ladies, and let me know when you have called for tea," he said as he departed.

With him gone, Georgiana continued to open up to Elizabeth. "My brother likes you, Miss Elizabeth," she said after he left.

"I like him too," Elizabeth replied with a smile. "You seem to have a very good brother."

Georgiana hesitated, glancing at where her brother had been sitting before lowering her gaze to her hands. She smoothed her skirt, her fingers twisting the fabric as she gathered the courage to speak. "I know he worries for me," she began softly, her voice barely above a whisper. "Because... because I do not always like to talk to strangers."

She paused, stealing a glance at Elizabeth before continuing, her words slow and deliberate, as though carefully choosing each one. "There were not many girls my age near Pemberley, and... and Father did not often invite guests. My cousins are all older, so I never had much company my own age." She swallowed, her voice faltering slightly. "My brother thought school would be good for me, and at first, I was glad to be among other girls. But... but none of them truly wished to be my friend."

Her fingers twisted tighter in her lap, her next words coming in a rush, as if saying them quickly might make it easier. "The ones who spoke to me only wanted introductions to my brother. Others tried to push me towards *their* brothers. And some ignored me entirely because—because even though my grandfather was an earl and my brother is wealthy, my father was untitled."

She took a steadying breath, lifting her gaze at last. "It felt as though no one cared for *me*, only for what I could offer them."

"It is unfortunate that was your experience there," Elizabeth said gently. "And, of course, your brother cannot introduce you to other young ladies your age, likely because he does not know any himself."

Georgiana nodded. "He has a few friends with whom he regularly spends time, but they are closer to him in age. If they have unmarried sisters, they are likely older than me and will also attempt to make use of the connection. He has one friend, Mr. Charles Bingley, and his sister has befriended me, but it is obvious that she only wants to encourage the friendship because she thinks I will push my brother towards her."

Elizabeth nodded, a little uncomfortable with such a topic so soon after meeting the girl, but it was apparent that she needed to speak about it with someone. Of course, the fact that Elizabeth was interested in her brother only made the feeling more pronounced.

"Miss Darcy, I would like to be your friend, but, well, this is awkward to say, but I also admire your brother. I do not know if anything will come of it, but I do not want to deceive you. However, I will say that regardless of what happens with your brother, I will still want to be your friend," she confessed after a moment.

"Oh, I already knew that, Miss Bennet," Georgiana said, speaking with more vigour than before. "It was clear from his request to introduce you to me that Brother is interested in you, and he told me how the two of you met. I also know he asked you to dance at my aunt's ball, but that I heard from the servants."

Elizabeth raised her brow at that. "Suddenly, my sense of what is right is warring with my curiosity to know what has been said. Surely you know you ought not to be listening to the gossip of servants," she said with a grin, and Georgiana quickly picked up on the tease.

"I usually do not, but this gossip was too interesting. My brother is known to avoid dancing, so for him to ask you for a dance more than a sennight before a ball, well, it is certainly indicative of something," Georgiana teased back. It was a successful tease, for Elizabeth's cheeks flamed.

The ice was broken between them, and the girls chatted for a full hour with Mrs. Gardiner and Mrs. Younge looking on. The former was pleased with how well the two were getting along, while the latter was most displeased. It did not serve her purposes for the girl to make a friend, especially not one like this Miss Bennet who would draw the shy girl out of her shell and, even worse, might embolden her to stand up for herself.

At the end of the hour, Georgiana called for tea and requested that her brother be notified. He joined them, and the two Darcy and their guests continued their pleasant visit. Mrs. Younge remained aloof, and before they departed, Mrs. Gardiner privately informed Darcy about what she had noticed.

"I will speak to Georgiana again, away from Mrs. Younge, to see what she has to say, and perhaps you can speak to your niece about my concerns as well. Will the two of you be able to return tomorrow?"

Mrs. Gardiner replied in the affirmative, and Darcy escorted the ladies to the waiting carriage. When he returned, he listened briefly at the door and heard Georgiana and Mrs. Younge talking, but he could not make out any of their words. He would continue to investigate and watch, and if all were not as it should be, he would sack the lady, uncaring what Lady Catherine might think.

Elizabeth became a fixture at Darcy House, calling on her new friend daily. They found much in common and soon addressed each other by their Christian names. Elizabeth's visits frequently began in the morning and lasted until the afternoon, so after the second visit on Friday, Mrs. Gardiner allowed Elizabeth to visit with a maid for company. The Gardiner carriage would convey her to Mayfair while the Darcy coach would bring her home.

The following Wednesday, the day before the St. Valentine's Day ball, Elizabeth and Georgiana were laughing and talking pleasantly with each other when they were surprised by the butler announcing a guest. "A Miss Caroline Bingley is asking if you are at home, Miss Darcy," he said, holding out a card.

"I am not at home to guests today, Morris. Please let her know that," Georgiana replied quietly.

"Miss Darcy," Mrs. Younge scolded. "Miss Bingley has been a good friend to your brother and to you. It is rude to refuse to see her."

"But, Mrs. Younge, Miss Bingley is not my friend. She only wants to try to see my brother. Elizabeth and I are having a lovely visit, and I do not want to wish it," Georgiana replied.

Mrs. Younge attempted to hide her anger and frustration at her charge's refusal of the lady, but Elizabeth saw a glimpse of it and was indignant on behalf of her friend. She did not care for the companion and had said as much to her aunt, but the way she overrode Miss Darcy's wishes in this matter and informed the butler to show the lady in was beyond the pale.

Resigned, Georgiana whispered a brief apology to Elizabeth and then seemed to ready herself to see her guest.

"Miss Darcy," the newcomer said, her voice condescending and insincere, "how lovely it is to see you."

"Miss Bingley," Georgiana replied. "I am surprised to see you today. My brother told me that he informed you I was not yet out, meaning that I could not accept callers unless he or my aunt were present and only by invitation. Why have you come?"

"Miss Darcy!" Mrs. Younge scolded.

"Miss Darcy!" Miss Bingley cried, clearly shocked at the young girl standing up to her. Then she noticed another person in the room, and her face reddened in mortification at realising there was a witness to her humiliating treatment by a *child*. That feeling quickly morphed into anger, and she turned it against the stranger.

Elizabeth stiffened at the sharp, disdainful tone as the woman before her sneered. "Who are you, and what are you doing here?" Her voice dripped with contempt. "I was certain I knew all of Miss Darcy's acquaintances, and if *I* am not permitted to visit, why on earth should *you* be?"

Her gaze raked over Elizabeth, assessing her attire with a practised eye. Though the quality of the fabric was beyond reproach, the design was less ostentatious than her own. But Miss Bingley had yet to learn that slavishly following the latest fashion did not always mean those designs would flatter the wearer.

Before Elizabeth could formulate a reply, a deep voice cut through the tense silence.

"*Miss Bingley!*"

Everyone turned at once. Mr. Darcy stood in the doorway, his expression thunderous.

"How dare you speak that way to a guest in my home?" His voice was calm, but the steel beneath it was unmistakable. "You do *not* know all of Georgiana's friends, nor do either of us owe you an explanation for our invitations. Particularly when you were explicitly told not to call without one."

His gaze locked onto Miss Bingley, cold and unyielding. "Why are you here?"

"Mr. Darcy," she said, attempting to placate the angry gentleman. "Why, I told you the other night when you dined with the family that I had been missing dear Georgiana. I assumed that you did not truly mean that I was only to call with an invitation and opted to take a chance that the two of you would be at home."

"Why would I tell you not to call if I did not mean it? And neither my sister nor I have permitted you to address her by her Christian name," Darcy stated, incredulous at her audacity.

"I cannot understand why you would not wish me to visit Geor...Miss Darcy. We are such good friends," Miss Bingley protested.

"No, we are not," Georgiana said, speaking up for the first time, causing Darcy to turn to her with a smile. "I asked my brother to keep you from calling on me. It is improper for you to call on me in the first place; you stay far longer than propriety dictates; and you only come so you can attempt to ensnare my brother. You spent your visits enquiring about my brother, suggesting changes to the decor, and speaking of what you would do as mistress, all while assuming I did not understand what you were attempting to do. Since I have no desire to have you as a sister, I wished to stop your visits entirely, but as usual, you did as you wanted and did not care what the other person might want or think."

Miss Bingley's mouth gaped open, looking very much like a freshly caught fish. Georgiana and Elizabeth held back their laughter until the lady was shown out by the footman who had accompanied Mr. Darcy. They hid their faces as they attempted to compose themselves.

"Miss Bennet, I am sorry you were subject to such a display," Darcy began, though his words were cut off by Mrs. Younge.

"Yes, Miss Darcy, I am quite ashamed of you. I am astounded that you could speak to a lady such as Miss Bingley in such a way. She may not be able to forgive you for such an insult, but you should write to her and apologise this instant. I will see your guests out," Mrs. Younge said, oblivious to the thunderous look her works caused in the master of the house.

"You will do nothing of the sort. My sister will not apologise to that woman after what she pulled today. I expressly forbade her from calling on my sister, yet she came anyway. While I would not wish my sister to need to speak to people in such a way often, I am proud of her for standing up for herself," Darcy retorted.

"Miss Darcy attempted to send the caller away, but Mrs. Younge insisted she be shown in," Elizabeth whispered to Darcy, who had moved to stand between her and Georgiana during the confrontation as if he wished to protect them both.

"What?" he bit out, turning towards Mrs. Younge and demanding an explanation.

"It was rude for her to deny her friend," she insisted.

"Miss Bingley is not her friend, and need I remind you that you are employed by me? I informed you weeks ago that Miss Bingley was not welcome here, and you apparently chose to ignore my wishes and those of my sister. I think it best that you pack your things immediately," Darcy replied.

"You cannot let me go in this manner," she protested.

"Perhaps Miss Bingley will help you find a position since you value her words more than mine," Darcy replied. "I expect you out of this house within the hour. A footman and maid will accompany you to your room to ensure nothing accidentally ends up in your trunks."

The door was not closed, so the butler surreptitiously called two servants to accompany the companion to her room. He would also stand guard and do what he could to assist the lady. As soon as Mrs. Younge left the room, Morris told Darcy he needed to speak to him. Darcy stepped into the hallway to talk to him.

"Mrs. Younge left the drawing room about fifteen minutes after you left Miss Darcy with her guests. She returned downstairs, stepping outside to hand what I thought was a note to someone. Miss Bingley let it slip that she knew Miss Darcy had guests, so I think Mrs. Younge may have been in contact with Miss Bingley," Morris whispered.

Darcy nodded, uncertain of what to do with this information. "Thank you, Morris. Let me know when she has left the house, and if you can, find out where she goes. I would not be surprised to learn she goes to Miss Bingley's house after what you have told me."

After taking a moment to rein in his anger, Darcy returned to his sister and guest. "Georgiana, I have asked you several times how you liked Mrs. Younge, but something tells me this is not the first time she has acted similarly. How often has she forced you to do as you bid, regardless of what you wanted?"

"It has become worse over the last week. She did not like my friendship with Elizabeth and was most vocal in criticising my friend. I intended to speak to you after the ball, but I did not want to say anything until then," Georgiana admitted.

"Why wait until after the ball?"

"I just felt it was important and did not want to add to your troubles before then," Georgiana replied, shrugging her shoulders.

Darcy looked at Elizabeth to see if she understood, but he did not pursue this further since she also looked confused.

"I will see what I can do about finding a new companion for you," Darcy said after a moment. "It is astonishing to me to learn that Mrs. Younge was in contact with Miss Bingley, though I do not know why I am surprised. Miss Bingley will go to any lengths to force me to notice her. She has certainly done so today; however, I doubt she will be pleased to have earned my notice this way. Bingley was invited to the ball, and his sister will undoubtedly accompany him, but I will not speak to her, much less dance with her. I will send him a note about her behaviour today, but if she approaches me, I will cut her."

Georgiana was slightly more shocked by this than Elizabeth, but it was Elizabeth who spoke. "Will this not harm your friend's reputation?"

"That is why I intend to warn him. If she does not approach me, no one will ever know. If I must cut her, it will be because of her actions," Darcy replied firmly.

Elizabeth could not challenge that reply and kept silent on the matter. After taking a few more moments to calm down, tea was ordered, and an hour later, Elizabeth was on her way home. She would not see Darcy again until the following night when he arrived at the Gardiners to escort them all to the ball.

CHAPTER 7

St. Valentine's Day Ball

In the week since being introduced to Georgiana, Elizabeth had visited Darcy House every day except St. Valentine's Day, the day of the ball at Matlock House. That morning, Elizabeth woke full of nerves, wishing, not for the first time, that she were at Longbourn. If for no other reason, Elizabeth longed for a long walk to try to work out her feelings. Being in town was lovely, but she missed the ability to walk out by herself and think.

She rose early and went downstairs to speak with her aunt and uncle. After confiding her need for a long walk, she was soon dressed warmly and sent to the park near the Gardiner's home, accompanied by a footman. There, she was given the time to walk off the anxiety she felt about the coming dance.

It was not the ball itself that concerned Elizabeth but the fact that she would be dancing the supper set with Mr. Darcy, which was sure to give rise to all manner of speculation. The thought of being the centre of attention—with all eyes on them—made her uneasy. She knew Mr. Darcy considered her worthy, but she was less confident about how the others would view her.

Over the past week, Elizabeth's friendship with Georgiana had flourished, and at the same time, her connection with Mr. Darcy had deepened. Each visit began with an hour or two spent alone with Georgiana, but Mr. Darcy joined them afterwards for conversation. Their discussions were lively and engaging, and when the afternoon visit ended, he never failed to escort Elizabeth home. A maid accompanied them in the carriage for propriety's sake, but their conversations flowed effortlessly despite the chaperone's presence.

They never seemed to run out of topics to discuss. Even when they disagreed, they found enjoyment in their debates, occasionally adopting opposing viewpoints simply to prolong the exchange. There was an ease between them, a growing familiarity that made each conversation more stimulating than the last.

Though it had only been about ten days since their initial meeting, Elizabeth was confident she was in love with Mr. Darcy. However, despite him honouring her with a dance that night, she had no idea how he felt about her. He had never spoken of courtship, nor had he given any indication that he might desire one. Elizabeth knew he was aware of her circumstances—particularly her lack of dowry—and perhaps he knew something of her family. Still, she was not sure if either of those things would deter him from considering her as a possible match.

To make matters worse, when Elizabeth returned home the previous day, she found a letter from her mother awaiting her. In it, Mrs. Bennet demanded her immediate return to Longbourn, declaring that Elizabeth did not deserve the 'reward' of remaining in London. Convinced that her daughter was enjoying herself too much, she had grown increasingly irritated by thinking of what she must be doing. In her view, Jane should be in town for the season, attending balls and parties and finding a suitor.

It mattered little that the Gardiners had yet to attend a single ball—the upcoming Matlock event being their first. Mrs. Bennet, imagining Elizabeth swept up in a flurry of social engagements, deemed it unfair that she should receive such favour. The letter left no room for argument: the Bennet carriage would arrive at the Gardiners' home by ten Monday morning to collect Elizabeth.

Elizabeth was conflicted. If she told Mr. Darcy and Georgiana she would be leaving in three days, they might miss her company, but their acquaintance would likely end there. She considered that Georgiana might write to her after she left, but Darcy—whatever feelings he might have had—would likely forget her once she was no longer in town. As she walked laps around the park, these thoughts weighed heavily on her, alongside her nerves about the evening.

After nearly an hour and a half of walking, the footman, struggling to keep pace, finally told Elizabeth it was time to return. "Miss Lizzy," he said, "your aunt and uncle have asked that I bring you back after no more than two hours. It has been nearly that long, and it is time to return." Elizabeth reluctantly agreed and followed him back to the Gardiners' home.

Once there, she spoke to her aunt. "Thank you for everything you have done for me these past months, especially for encouraging my relationship with the Darcys. As you know, Mama wrote to me yesterday, and though I did not mention the contents of the letter before, I must tell you now. She insists I return home as soon as possible. The letter states the Bennet carriage will arrive on Monday to return me to Longbourn.

Jane is to stay in London in my place and attend events with you, since, apparently, I do not deserve such attention. She also said that since it is unlikely that I will ever catch a husband, Jane should come here to find one to, as she puts it, 'save the family.'"

Mrs. Gardiner sympathised with Elizabeth but knew she could not defy her sister-in-law's wishes. It seemed strange that Mrs. Bennet would send Jane to London without an invitation, as if she expected Jane to take Elizabeth's place without question. While Mrs. Gardiner was tempted to send Jane back with Elizabeth, she decided it would be best to discuss the matter with her husband before making any decisions.

Darcy prepared for the evening across town at Darcy House, though his uncertainty was for an entirely different reason. Tonight, he would ask Elizabeth Bennet to enter into a courtship. His feelings for her had only deepened over the past ten days, and with each passing moment in her company, Darcy had grown more certain—Elizabeth was unlike any woman he had ever met and was on a fair way to claiming his heart. For the first time in memory, he was looking forward to attending a ball, knowing that the prospect of dancing the supper set with her would make the evening not only bearable but enjoyable.

Darcy had always avoided opening a ball with a partner, wary of raising expectations he had no intention of fulfilling. But tonight, he also intended to claim Elizabeth for the first set. Initially, he had refrained from securing a second dance with her, uncertain where their acquaintance would lead. Now, however, he wished to make his interest unmistakable. Not only would he lead her out for the first and supper dances, but he also hoped to stir speculation among those in attendance.

Let them speculate. For once, Darcy was prepared to meet and exceed expectations.

With this thought in mind, Darcy stepped into his carriage for the journey across town to Gracechurch Street. Gardiner had, at first, insisted that his escorting them was unnecessary, but when Darcy had visited the warehouse to speak to him earlier that day, he had agreed to the escort, along with the promise of a few minutes alone with Elizabeth to make his request.

Conversely, Darcy's journey to the Gardiners was too short and too long. He was anxious to see his Elizabeth again, for that was how he referred to her in his mind, but he was also nervous that she might reject him. Darcy believed she cared for him and liked him, but she was uncertain how she would respond to his request for courtship and for a second significant set at the ball.

Gardiner had told Darcy a bit more about Elizabeth's family that afternoon, including how Mrs. Bennet constantly criticised Elizabeth and her insistence that Elizabeth would never marry. Darcy scoffed at the idea but also understood how being treated in such an infamous way by her mother could affect a young woman. He would do all he could to bolster Elizabeth's thoughts about herself and show her, in word and deed, how much she meant to him.

The housekeeper showed Darcy directly to Gardiner's study. "I am afraid I have news for you," Gardiner began, handing the younger man a glass of port.

"Is Miss Elizabeth well?" Darcy asked, having been asked to call her that earlier in the week when she was with his sister.

"Physically, she is well, but her mother wrote to her yesterday demanding that she return home. She did not say anything to her aunt until this morning, and I did not learn of it until I arrived. I do not know how this will affect your resolve to court her, but I know the thought of leaving the company of you and your sister troubles her," Gardiner replied.

Darcy took a sip of his drink, taking a moment to think the matter over. "Would her father allow her to stay in London if I asked?"

"I cannot say. Bennet is not one to stand against his wife, which is why Lizzy has remained with us for as long as she has. He might prefer she return home simply because he may think you would give up your pursuit of her if she was there," Gardiner replied honestly.

"And I were to propose marriage instead? I know what I want but am uncertain of Miss Elizabeth's feelings," Darcy replied.

"My wife would know better than I," Gardiner said. "But perhaps the best solution is to allow you and Lizzy ten minutes alone so the two of you might discuss the matter. I believe the ladies are ready now; I will send her to you here."

Darcy nodded, and both men stood. A few minutes later, Elizabeth entered the room, and Darcy was momentarily speechless when he saw her in her ivory dress, trimmed with an emerald green ribbon that matched her eyes.

"You look beautiful, Elizabeth," he breathed.

She felt her cheeks heat both at his compliment and his use of her Christian name. "Thank you, Mr. Darcy," she murmured.

"Elizabeth, when I arrived tonight, I intended to ask you for a courtship. However, after speaking to your uncle and seeing how lovely you look, well, I have changed my mind," he said.

Elizabeth's head dropped, and Darcy saw the tears pool at the corner of her eyes. "No," he rushed to say, stepping towards her and taking her hands in his. "No, no, it is not what you think. My darling Elizabeth, I do not wish to ask for a mere courtship. I want to ask you to be my wife. A courtship would have allowed us to get to know each other more, perhaps, but we can learn about each other during our engagement as easily. I do not need a courtship to tell me that you are the only woman I desire to be my wife, my partner."

"Truly?" Elizabeth asked, looking at him for the first time that evening.

"Truly," came the earnest reply. "Elizabeth, will you marry me? We can go to the ball tonight and announce our engagement. Your uncle is your guardian and can permit us to do so. I can go to your father tomorrow to ask him to allow you to stay, but even if he does not, I will find a way to come to you. Georgiana can lease a home for a month or two until the wedding. If we are already engaged and must be separated for a time, we can write to each other."

"What if my father objects?" Elizabeth asked.

"Do you think he will?" Darcy questioned, wondering what sort of man might reject such an eligible suitor, but Gardiner had told him before that Thomas Bennet was not like many men.

"I cannot say for certain," Elizabeth replied, turning away from him slightly as she thought about him making the journey to Longbourn. "I almost hate the thought of you meeting my family and having to speak to any of them. If my mother knew of your request, she would not let him refuse you based on your wealth alone. I have been to your house, sir, and know you are well off, even if I do not know the particulars. However, she will try to convince you that you should marry Jane instead."

"I love you, Elizabeth, and not even Aphrodite herself could dissuade me from marrying you," Darcy declared. "You are beautiful, no matter what your mother may say, and even if your sister were Helen of Troy, I would not trade your wit and conversation for all the silent beauties in the world."

Elizabeth looked up at him with that crooked brow he had learned to recognise as the prelude to a tease. "You would not cast me aside were Aphrodite or Helen to appear and be willing to follow you home?" she asked, her lips curving into a mischievous smile.

Darcy chuckled, shaking his head. "Not even if they begged on bended knee."

Elizabeth laughed. "Aphrodite, begging? Now that I should like to see."

"You are the only goddess I have eyes for," he said softly, reaching for her hand. "No myth or legend could compare to the woman before me."

Elizabeth's teasing expression softened, and she simply gazed at him for a moment. Then, giving his hand a gentle squeeze, she whispered, "Then I am the most fortunate of women. Yes, Mr. Darcy, I will marry you. If Father will not consent, well, if he will not, we will do whatever we must."

Leaning down, Darcy captured her lips in a slow, lingering kiss, his hand sliding up to cradle her cheek. "I love you," he murmured against her lips, his voice husky with emotion.

"Not as much as I love you," she whispered, her gaze full of teasing and challenge.

A wicked gleam entered Darcy's eyes. "Is that so?" he murmured before claiming her lips again, this time more urgently. His arms tightened around her, drawing her flush against him as he deepened the kiss, leaving no room for doubt as to the depth of his devotion.

When they finally parted, breathless and dazed, Elizabeth laughed softly, her forehead resting against his. "Perhaps it is best we inform my aunt and uncle of our news. And we still have a ball to attend."

"We do, and now that we are engaged, I must claim more of your dances," he said, his voice warm with affection. "I have already secured the supper, but I wish for your first and final sets as well." His fingers brushed lightly over hers, his gaze unwavering. "I have never anticipated a ball as much as I do tonight. Though my aunt will no doubt insist I stand up with one or two others, know that my thoughts will never stray far from you—nor from the joy of knowing that you have made me the happiest of men."

The couple's news was met with hearty congratulations from Elizabeth's aunt and uncle and, later, by Darcy's family. Lord and Lady Matlock, already acquainted with Elizabeth, received the announcement with approval. Lady Matlock had always wished for Darcy to find a woman who could match his intellect and spirit and was especially delighted by his choice.

When Lord Matlock heard the news, he let out a hearty laugh. Elizabeth was not only poised and well-spoken but also a formidable chess player who had challenged—and occasionally bested—him. "She will certainly keep you on your toes, Darcy," he remarked with amusement. "You shall have to work to keep up with her."

To his surprise, his nephew did not bristle at the tease. Instead, Darcy merely smiled—a rare, unguarded expression that spoke volumes about his feelings for the lady in question.

As expected, Darcy opening the ball with an unknown young lady incited much speculation amongst those in attendance that night. Some initially assumed she must be a distant relation or a guest of Lady Matlock's since she had arrived with Darcy. Others, noting his usual reluctance to dance, suspected there was more to the matter. But the whispers grew louder when he also claimed her for the supper set. Who was this dark-haired beauty at his side?

As they moved gracefully through the steps of the dance, Elizabeth arched a teasing brow at him. "You do realise you have set the entire room to whispering, sir?"

Darcy's lips quirked. "Let them whisper. I have nothing to be ashamed of. If I could, I would declare to the entire room that I have found my perfect match."

Elizabeth tilted her head playfully. "Nothing at all? Not even the smallest regret at connecting yourself to an unknown country miss?"

He met her gaze, his expression softening. "I regret nothing and am rather enjoying being the object of speculation for once. They are all wondering how you have captured me and do not know that it was I who have won the prize."

She laughed, the sound warm and bright. "Who are you, and what have you done with Fitzwilliam Darcy?"

"I have merely decided to embrace what I have always known to be true," he said, his voice quieter now. "That you are the only woman I have ever wished to dance with."

A blush rose in Elizabeth's cheeks, but she did not look away. Instead, she lightly squeezed his hand as the dance brought them together again.

As the night went on, many guests sought introductions, determined to uncover the identity of the woman who had so completely captivated Darcy. Gentlemen were drawn to her charm, while disappointed mamas and envious debutantes scrutinised her with a critical eye. They whispered about her lack of noble connections—no one seemed to know her—and murmured over the simplicity of her gown. Yet even the sharpest tongues could find little fault with the fine fabric and elegant cut. Most of all, they could not ignore the exquisite attention Darcy lavished upon her throughout the evening.

As the strains of the final notes faded and he led her back to her seat, Darcy leaned in slightly. "Would you grant me your final dance, my love?"

Elizabeth pretended to consider, then smiled archly. "Since you have already danced more than usual, one more would hardly damage your reputation further."

And when he led her out for a third set, the entire room seemed to come to the same conclusion. Though no formal announcement had been made, nor had any connection been publicly acknowledged, it was undeniable—the elusive, much sought-after bachelor from Derbyshire had been caught.

CHAPTER 8

Returning Home

After discussing it with Gardiner, Darcy waited until Saturday to ride to Longbourn to ask Elizabeth's father for her hand and permission for her to remain an additional week in London.

As expected, Mr. Bennet gave his daughter's suitor a difficult time. Eventually, he agreed to both requests, although informing Mrs. Bennet of the new arrangements proved to be every bit as difficult as Elizabeth had indicated.

When Mr. Bennet introduced Darcy to his wife, he simply referred to him as their daughter's suitor, neglecting to specify which daughter. Mrs. Bennet, believing the young man had somehow heard of Jane's beauty and had come to seek her attention, was on the verge of scolding her husband—until her sharp eyes took in the stranger's attire.

"Well, this is quite unusual, sir, but I am certain that my beautiful daughter Jane would be delighted to meet you. Do you intend to remain in the area for long?" Mrs. Bennet gushed.

"I am not here to meet any of your daughters, madam. I am engaged to your second daughter, Elizabeth. Your husband has just given us his permission to marry in six weeks, and she will remain in London for another week or two to order her trousseau and for me to arrange a place for my sister and me to stay while we wait for the wedding to take place," Darcy said.

"But you have not yet met my Jane," Mrs. Bennet cried. "When you see her, you will understand that she is a far better prospect for a bride. Lizzy is nothing to her."

"I will gladly meet all my future sisters, but Elizabeth is my choice. Your daughter Jane may be lovely, but she is not the one I love," Darcy replied while Bennet watched, amused at the tableau before him.

Mrs. Bennet looked at him, perplexed. "Then I will accompany you back to London to help Elizabeth shop for her wedding clothes. Her aunt will not know how to assist her best; I know far better what is required."

"I rode from London, Mrs. Bennet," Darcy said. "Elizabeth and Mrs. Gardiner have already arranged with my sister's *modiste* to begin her trousseau, and my aunt, Lady Matlock, will also assist her with her choices. There is no need for you to come as well."

"But the wedding," Mrs. Bennet cried. "Six weeks is not nearly long enough to plan such a grand event as will be necessary. Oh, do you mean to say you are related to an earl and his countess? Will they attend the wedding? No, six weeks is far too short; six months would be better."

"No, madam, the wedding will take place in six weeks. I must return to my estate for the spring planting and can delay no longer. Neither Elizabeth nor I wish to wait so long to wed, nor do we wish to be separated for such a length of time,"

Darcy replied, his tone firm and allowing no room for argument. "If you cannot make the necessary arrangements here, my aunt can see to everything in London, and we shall marry there instead. Of course, in that case, it is unlikely your family could attend..."

He let the words hang in the air, allowing the full weight of the possibility to settle in Mrs. Bennet's mind.

The prospect of being excluded at last forced Mrs. Bennet to relent. It was agreed that Elizabeth would return home within a fortnight and the wedding would occur at the end of March. Darcy and Elizabeth would settle on a precise date and inform Mr. and Mrs. Bennet upon their arrival at Longbourn when they returned.

It took the couple ten days to accomplish what was needed. On the twenty-sixth of February, Elizabeth returned to Longbourn after two months away, arriving in the Darcy carriage along with her intended and Georgiana.

The Great House at Stoke was available to let for the month required to plan the wedding, and Darcy arranged with Mr. Philips to lease it for the duration. Lord and Lady Matlock intended to come with their youngest son and a few of Darcy's friends the week before the wedding. They would all stay at the leased estate and return to London immediately following the wedding breakfast.

Though Mrs. Bennet still attempted, on occasion, to push Darcy towards one of her other daughters, it took only a pointed look from him to silence her efforts. It seemed she had not forgotten his threat to have the wedding in London should she misbehave. That did not, however, stop her from complaining to her friends and neighbours about the rushed nature of the wedding and the lack of finery as a result. She bemoaned the fact that Jane had not had the same opportunity as Elizabeth to meet eligible men in town, but she never voiced these sentiments when Darcy was nearby.

During this period, the engaged couple often indulged in long walks, most frequently accompanied by Georgiana and Mary. The two young women, only a few years apart in age, quickly found much in common and soon formed a close bond.

One afternoon, as they walked along a shaded path, Georgiana glanced at Elizabeth before turning to her brother. "Fitzwilliam, I have been thinking... Mary and I get along so well. Would it be permissible for her to visit Pemberley after the wedding?"

Elizabeth smiled at her sister. "That is a lovely idea, Georgiana, but it is not for me to decide."

Darcy regarded his sister thoughtfully. "You are quite determined on this, are you?"

"Oh yes," Georgiana said eagerly. "She is clever and well-read, and she loves music. We would be excellent companions for one another."

Darcy glanced at Elizabeth, whose eyes shone with approval. With a slight nod, he said, "Then it shall be so. Mary, would you like to visit Pemberley?"

Caught off guard, Mary blinked in surprise. "Oh! I—I would like that very much, sir."

"Then it is settled," Darcy said, offering Elizabeth his arm.

Georgiana beamed, and Elizabeth gave Mary's hand a reassuring squeeze. As they continued their walk, the conversation turned to Derbyshire, and soon, even Mary could not help but look forward to what was to come.

"When our aunt arrives, she will bring a companion for you, Georgiana," Darcy said. "Richard approves of her, and so does Aunt Matlock, but you must tell me what you think of the lady. She will help guide you as you prepare to enter society, and Mary, you may also benefit from her company."

Mary beamed at being included in this, for she had often felt lost as the middle child with so many sisters and said as much to Darcy.

A week before the wedding, just before the Matlocks were scheduled to arrive with Fitzwilliam, Jane approached Elizabeth to request a favour. "You and Mr. Darcy are going to London for your honeymoon, are you not? Will you spend the rest of the season in town?"

"No, we will not," Elizabeth replied. "We will spend our wedding night at the house he has leased but will travel soon after that to Pemberley. Fitzwilliam wishes to be at his estate for the spring planting and to ensure that all is in order."

"Oh," Jane replied blankly, having believed her mother's claims about the couple's plans. "But would you not prefer to spend some time in town, obtaining your trousseau and attending balls and other fetes given in your honour?"

"No, Jane, I would not, and neither would Fitzwilliam. We attended one ball the entire time I was in London and went to the theatre once. I have told you that the Gardiners do not attend such events often, and Fitzwilliam is not fond of such amusements."

"I had hoped you would ask me to join you in town," Jane tried. "You owe me that after costing me a suitor in the autumn."

Elizabeth sighed heavily at the direction this conversation had gone. "I owe you nothing, Jane. At your insistence, I accompanied you on walks with that man, and because you would not talk, you asked me to engage him in conversation. That he was such a fool to have insulted us both as he did was not a mark of gentlemanly behaviour. Would you truly have wished to be tied to such a man?"

"I would have been married, the mistress of Netherfield, and no longer living at home," Jane retorted. "It would have been all I could have wanted."

"Then I am sorry that he did not offer for you, but do not blame me for your unwillingness to engage him in conversation. Perhaps, had you spoken, he would have offered for you. However, what is done is done, and I cannot change what is past," Elizabeth replied before excusing herself and returning to her room.

To the neighbours' surprise, Mary stood up with Elizabeth at the wedding. After their discussion a few days before, Jane did not seek her sister out again, but those gathered noted her absence but did not remark upon it. Mary, too, eventually accompanied her sister to Derbyshire, where she remained with Georgiana, forging a quiet but steadfast friendship with the younger girl.

The wedding breakfast at Longbourn was far more modest than Mrs. Bennet might have wished, but it perfectly reflected the couple's tastes. The guests from London found the gathering entirely fitting for Elizabeth and Darcy, who had no desire for ostentation or any need to impress. They wished only to celebrate their marriage in the company of those they held dear.

Although Mrs. Bennet had grumbled about not being able to make the plans as she wished, her spirits lifted when the Countess of Matlock approached her after the ceremony. "Mrs. Bennet," she said warmly, "I must commend you. You have planned everything carefully and, more importantly, with the bride and groom's wishes at heart. It is rare to see a wedding so perfectly suited to those it honours."

Mrs. Bennet blinked, uncertain for a moment whether she had heard correctly. "Oh! Well, I did wish for something grander, of course, but Lizzy can be most determined when she sets her mind to something. I would have much preferred they waited until the autumn to marry."

The countess inclined her head. "Determination is an admirable quality in a young lady, particularly when it leads to the happiness of so many. And, as I am sure you must agree, Mrs. Darcy looked happy indeed."

At this, Mrs. Bennet preened. "Yes, yes, she did, did she not?" Her gaze flitted to where Elizabeth stood with Darcy, their hands entwined as they spoke softly to the Gardiners. "I daresay you are right, Lady Matlock. And what is more important than a daughter's happiness?"

The countess smiled. "Indeed."

And so, though Mrs. Bennet had not had the grand spectacle she had envisioned, she took comfort knowing that she had, at least, arranged a wedding worthy of the praise of a countess.

Epilogue

After their marriage, Darcy and Elizabeth enjoyed a sennight of peace in the Great House at Stoke. Their guests departed for London after the wedding breakfast, with Georgiana and Mary accompanying Lord and Lady Matlock.

As Georgiana's other guardian, Colonel Fitzwilliam escorted the young ladies back to Darcy at the end of the week. Once reunited, the entire party embarked on their journey north to Pemberley.

From the moment Elizabeth first beheld Pemberley, she knew she would love it. The house, grand yet harmonious with its surroundings, seemed to have risen naturally from the landscape. Though the beauty of the estate was undeniable, it was the parkland that truly captured her heart. The vast, rolling grounds, with their winding streams and ancient trees, beckoned her to explore.

Throughout the first summer of their marriage, Darcy and Elizabeth traversed every part of the estate, first by leisurely walks and carriage rides. However, it did not take long for

Darcy to persuade Elizabeth to learn to ride, a skill she soon came to enjoy. With this newfound freedom, she ventured farther than ever, delighting in the ever-changing beauty of the land she now called home.

Her explorations, however, became more limited as autumn turned to winter. Six months after their wedding, Elizabeth began to suspect she was with her child. Her suspicions were joyfully confirmed shortly after the new year when she first felt the quickening. The following spring, with the gardens of Pemberley in full bloom, the heir to Pemberley was welcomed into the world, bringing even greater happiness to the couple's already blissful union.

The couple visited Longbourn only rarely. They occasionally received letters from Elizabeth's family, but more often than not, these letters contained demands for gifts of gowns, ribbons, trips to town, introductions to their connections, basically anything Mrs. Bennet felt she or her favourite daughters deserved. Jane also wrote, making similar requests, although Kitty and Lydia rarely bothered. At first, Elizabeth responded to these letters, kindly declining the requests, but she eventually grew tired of them. The letters were then refused or consigned to the fire unread.

Mr. Bennet could scarcely be bothered to write to his once favourite daughter himself, although the steward still occasionally wrote to her to ask her or her husband's advice on a matter when the master could not be troubled. After consulting with Darcy, Elizabeth did respond to these only because she did not wish to see the tenants she had long cared for in a bad situation.

There was only one instance where the Darcys' life in town intersected with that of the Bennets.

Having heard Darcy mention it in passing in reference to his bride's home, Bingley decided to lease the estate of Netherfield. Their friendship, however, was never the same as it had once been. Caroline Bingley, still smarting from her treatment at Darcy House and the subsequent denial of Darcy's permission to visit or use his name to gain social invitations, had not forgiven the slight. She had attempted to reclaim her position by appearing on her brother's arm at the Matlocks' St. Valentine's Day ball. Despite Darcy's explicit warnings, she had approached him—and, as promised, he had cut her publicly and definitively, ensuring her ruin in society.

Seeking to escape the social consequences of his sister's disgrace, Bingley resolved to leave London and discovered that Netherfield was available to let. Hoping that proximity to Darcy might help mend their fractured friendship, he took the house. Though she despised the area, Miss Bingley accompanied her brother as his hostess and soon found an unlikely alliance with the Bennet family. She recognised that Mrs. Bennet was eager for news of her most successful daughter and, in turn, used the connection to glean whatever details she could about the new Mrs. Darcy.

Jane, for her part, saw an opportunity in Miss Bingley's growing interest. Aware of the woman's true motives, she nonetheless cultivated the acquaintance, using it to gain access to Bingley himself. It did not take long for her to secure his attentions, and before the year was out, he had proposed. Mrs. Bennet could at last host the grand wedding she had always desired.

Bingley and his sister were taken aback when the Darcys did not attend the wedding. Only then did they come to understand the actual state of affairs. Jane had led them to believe that she and Elizabeth were in frequent correspondence, fostering the impression of a warm sisterly relationship. It was a shock to discover that their exchanges had been infrequent, civil but distant, and that Mr. and Mrs. Darcy wished little to do with the Bennet family—Jane most of all.

However, by the time this realisation dawned, it was far too late. The marriage contracts had been signed, and the vows exchanged. Whatever deception the new Mrs. Bingley had employed to secure her position, it was not grounds for annulment. Whether the couple were happy was uncertain, and since Miss Bingley remained unwed, she lived with them throughout their marriage.

Acknowledgments

I have an incredible group of people who support me and my writing. Of course, my family is who allows me to spend far too much of my time sitting in front of my computer. But many others provide assistance in so many ways. I thank you all.

About the Author

Melissa Anne first read Pride and Prejudice in high school and discovered the world of JAFF a few years ago. After reading quite a few, she thought perhaps she could do that, and began writing, first on fan fiction sites, and then published as an independent author. Melissa Anne is a pen name.

She began her career as a newspaper reporter before becoming a middle school English teacher and then a high school English teacher. She lives and works in Georgia, although she grew up in East Tennessee and claims that as home. Melissa has been married to a rather wonderful man (something of a cross between a Darcy and a Bingley) for two decades, and they have three children.

Contact her at melissa.anne.author@gmail.com

Be the first to know when Melissa Anne's next book is available! Follow her at https://www.bookbub.com/authors/melissa-anne *to get an alert whenever she has a new release, preorder, or discount!*

Want to read snippets of Melissa's Works in Progress? Check out her Substack here: https://melissaanneauthor.substack.com/

- facebook.com/melissa.anne.author
- instagram.com/melissa.anne.author
- bookbub.com/profile/melissa-anne
- amazon.com/stores/Melissa-Anne/author/B0C54C1BNF
- youtube.com/@MelissaAnneAuthor

Also by Melissa Anne

Regency Pride and Prejudice Variations

In Spite of All

When Love is True

Darcy & Elizabeth's Dreams of Redemption

Worthy of Her Trust

Hearts Entwined

Responsibility and Resentment

A Different Impression

What Happened After Lambton

The Accidental Letter (novella)

Holidays With Darcy and Elizabeth

A Return at Christmas (short story)

Darcy and Elizabeth's Valentine's Meet Cute (short story)

Modern Variations

Finding Love at Loch Ness

Printed in Great Britain
by Amazon